Her heart pounding, Dee cautiously pulled herself forward on the branch. She had to get a closer look at the intruder. She gripped the branch with both hands and stared into the window. What she saw made her gasp.

A girl crossed in front of the bed. Dee saw that she had pale, pale skin and a small oval face framed by long auburn ringlets. She was wearing a puff-sleeved white blouse with a high collar under a long black pinafore.

What is she dressed up for—a part in Little Women? Dee asked herself.

The girl picked up Dee's Walkman and began fiddling with the buttons as if she wasn't quite sure how to work it. When the cassette holder popped open, she dropped the Walkman on the bed in surprise.

"This is too much!" Dee muttered aloud. "Wait till Aunt Winnifred learns there's another girl hiding in the—"

What Dee saw next made her stop in midsentence. Her mouth dropped open, and she nearly lost her grip on the tree branch.

The girl had vanished into thin air!

Frozen with fear, Dee hugged the branch tighter.

The girl in her bedroom wasn't a girl—she was a ghost!

Bantam Skylark Books of related interest
Ask your bookseller for the books you have missed

ANNE OF GREEN GABLES by L. M. Montgomery
ANNIE AND THE ANIMALS by Barbara Beasley Murphy
THE CASTLE IN THE ATTIC by Elizabeth Winthrop
DAPHNE'S BOOK by Mary Downing Hahn
FELITA by Nicholosa Mohr
THE GHOST IN THE THIRD ROW by Bruce Coville
THE GHOST WORE GRAY by Bruce Coville
GOING HOME by Nicholasa Mohr
THE PICOLINIS by Anne Graham Estern
THE PICOLINIS AND THE HAUNTED HOUSE
   by Anne Graham Estern
TIME AT THE TOP by Edward Ormondroyd
THE TROLLEY TO YESTERDAY by John Bellairs
ZUCCHINI by Barbara Dana

The Ghost in the Attic

Emily Cates

A BANTAM SKYLARK BOOKS

NEW YORK • TORONTO • LONDON • SYDNEY • AUCKLAND

RL 4, 008–012

THE GHOST IN THE ATTIC
A Bantam Skylark Book / October 1990

Skylark Books is a registered trademark of Bantam Books, a division of Bantam Doubleday Dell Publishing Group, Inc. Registered in U.S. Patent and Trademark Office and elsewhere.

Published by arrangement with Parachute Press, Inc.

All rights reserved.
Copyright © 1990 by Parachute Press, Inc.
Cover art copyright © 1990 by Garin Baker.
Designed by GDS / Jeffrey L. Ward
No part of this book may be reproduced or transmitted in any form or by any means, electronic or mechanical, including photocopying, recording, or by any information storage and retrieval system, without permission in writing from the publisher.
For information address: Bantam Books.

ISBN 0-553-15826-0

Published simultaneously in the United States and Canada

Bantam Books are published by Bantam Books, a division of Bantam Doubleday Dell Publishing Group, Inc. Its trademark, consisting of the words "Bantam Books" and the portrayal of a rooster, is Registered in U.S. Patent and Trademark Office and in other countries. Marca Registrada. Bantam Books, 666 Fifth Avenue, New York, New York 10103.

PRINTED IN THE UNITED STATES OF AMERICA

OPM   0 9 8 7 6 5 4 3 2 1

Many thanks to Suzanne Weyn
for developing the original concept of
Haunting with Louisa

CHAPTER

1

"Watch your step, miss."

Dee Forest grabbed the side of the small ferry boat that had brought her in from the mainland. She steadied herself for a moment, then climbed onto the wooden dock. A gust of cold wind nearly blew her back into the boat, which was bobbing in the rough waters below.

Mr. Spalding, the ferry captain, handed up her two suitcases, one at a time. "I'm sure your Aunt Winnifred will be along real soon," he said. "She'll be happy for the company, I'll bet. Don't get many visitors to Misty Island after Labor Day."

Dee's eyes narrowed as she scanned the gray,

rocky beach and peered down at the old, deserted lighthouse on the jetty. "No, I guess not," she said uncertainly.

"You ever been to the island before?" Spalding asked.

"Yes, but not since I was three," Dee said. She had to shout over the gusting wind. Ocean spray drenched her face and hair. A gray cloud drifted quickly over the sun, and Dee watched its dark shadow roll over the beach.

"It gets quiet after all the summer people go home," Spalding went on. "Real quiet." He pulled his flannel jacket tighter around him. "Guess I'd better be heading back. There's a storm brewing for sure. Don't worry. Your aunt'll be along."

"I'll by okay," Dee said, shivering. "Thanks again for the lift."

"My regards to your aunt. Enjoy your stay," Spalding called. The little boat spun around, kicking up a white, frothy whirlpool in the dark ocean waters.

Dee watched for a few seconds as Spalding sped back toward the mainland. Then, feeling the sharp, cold wind even through her heavy wool fisherman's sweater, she picked up her suitcases and carried them down to the rocky shore.

"Enjoy your stay." Mr. Spalding's words echoed in her mind.

Dee sighed. This wasn't exactly a pleasure trip for her.

Her hand went up to the pendant around her neck—a sleek, silver dove, its wings spread in graceful flight. The pendant had belonged to Dee's mother. And it was all Dee had left of her.

Her mother had died in a car crash at the beginning of the summer. Dee missed her terribly. But as long as Dee wore the silver dove, she could still feel her mother's presence.

"I'll never remove the pendant," Dee had vowed to herself. "Never."

The summer had been one of shock—and of sorrow. Normally energetic and outgoing, Dee had spent day after day alone in her room, mourning her mother and waiting for the tears to stop.

Then one day in August, she'd told her father, "I'm finished crying, Dad. I'm all cried out."

"And how do you feel now?" Mr. Forest had

asked, running a hand through his thinning blond hair.

"Lonely," Dee had said. "Like I lost my best friend."

Her father had stared at the wall, his eyes sad and dreamy. He hadn't said anything then, but a few days later he'd announced his plan for her.

"But *why* do I have to go live with Aunt Winnifred?" Dee had protested. "My friends are all here in Cambridge."

"You haven't seen your friends all summer," her father'd reminded her gently. "You need a change, Dee. A complete change."

"Okay. I'll go upstairs and change!" Dee had exclaimed. She'd been surprised to realize that her sharp tongue and sense of humor seemed to be returning.

Dee had expected her father to laugh—or at least smile—but Mr. Forest had looked as sad as ever. "Let's be honest," he had said. "*I'm* the one who needs the change. I've got to get away from this house—these memories—at least for a while. I'm sorry, honey, but I've decided to take a job down in Brockton. It will only be for a few months. Then I'll join you and Aunt Win on Misty Island."

Dee had been about to protest again, but one look at her father's unhappy face had stopped her, making her decide not to fight him any longer.

"Your aunt will take good care of you," Mr. Forest had continued. "I'm sure you'll be—"

"That's okay, Dad," Dee had interrupted. "I understand." And she had.

After that, Dee had little time for arguments or emotional scenes. She'd been too busy shopping, packing, and saying tearful good-byes to her friends. And then there had been the countless calls to Misty Island to make sure Aunt Winnifred would be ready for her and enroll her in school.

School.

What kind of junior high could they possibly have on Misty Island? Dee had wondered. It would probably be a one-room schoolhouse with desks nailed to the floor, quill pens and inkwells, and a teacher who hit kids' hands with a ruler when they spoke out of turn!

Dee had worried about the school. She'd worried about living with Aunt Winnifred, who had always been considered a bit of a character. She'd worried about living on a lonely tourist island after all the tourists had left for the winter. And, most of all, she had worried about her dad—how would he manage without her?

Dee had never revealed any of her worries, though. After the first argument, she hadn't said a word of complaint to her father. She'd decided to make the best of things.

It was only for the winter, after all.

And now, here she was—watching the foamy waves tumble and crash against the low, wooden dock. She felt the ice-cold spray on her face and the wet chunks of sand beneath her yellow high-top sneakers.

At the end of the beach, the old lighthouse on the jetty almost disappeared behind the rising mists. The clouds thickened again over the sun. The winds howled across the sand as the beach grew darker and the low sky became tinged with an eerie green.

This place is definitely creepy, Dee thought—just a moment before a powerful hand grabbed her shoulder from behind.

Dee's scream echoed off the shadowed sea cliffs and into the wind.

CHAPTER
2

"I'm so sorry. I didn't mean to startle you," Winnifred Forest said. "I would have been on time. Only there was a mix-up with my calendar."

"Your calendar?" Dee was puzzled. "You mean you had another appointment?"

"No. I was looking at the wrong month. Would you believe I still had August up? No wonder things have seemed strange these past few weeks!"

Dee laughed. Aunt Win was definitely a character. Dee had a feeling that living with her aunt was not going to be dull.

"Anyway, I'm sorry to be late," Aunt Win said, looking Dee up and down. "I finally discovered my mistake this morning. So I *knew* today was the day you were arriving. I was all set for you. I even left the house early."

"And?"

"And the jeep got stuck. Four-wheel drive, and it gets stuck in the driveway. What a disgrace!"

Dee laughed. The beach seemed to brighten a bit, the pale sand shimmering silver and gold. She studied her aunt. Winnifred had to be at least sixty. But she had bright orange hair, obviously dyed, and wore bright orange lipstick to match. She was a large woman with strong, oversized hands and broad shoulders.

Aunt Win moved with the sprightliness of a much younger person. She was dressed in baggy, green corduroy slacks, patched at both knees. And despite the autumn chill, she wore only a lightweight gray sweatshirt with the words *Misty Island Inn* written across the front in faded maroon letters.

"Hey—you've grown," she said, as if surprised.

"Well, I hope so, Aunt Win," Dee said. "I was only a child the last time you saw me. I'm thirteen now."

"That isn't too old to give your aunt a hug, is it?" Winnifred asked, grinning.

Dee returned the grin and stepped forward to hug her.

"I know this must be hard for you," Aunt Win said softly, wrapping her arms around her niece. Dee felt the tears welling up in her eyes, but she blinked them back.

"Well, you look frozen through and through," Aunt Win said. "Let's load your suitcases in the jeep and get to the inn so we can warm up. Good idea?"

"Good idea," Dee agreed, shivering as the wind picked up off the ocean. She reached for her suitcases, but Win was faster. The big woman hoisted the heavy bags as if they were weightless, and began marching quickly over the wet sand.

Dee took one look at the jeep at the edge of the beach and yelped in dismay. "Aunt Win! It's freezing out here. Where's the top to the jeep?"

"I have no idea," her aunt called back. "I haven't used that thing in years. I like to smell the sea air when I drive."

A few seconds later, the topless jeep was speeding over the narrow, twisting road, past the wooded dunes, and toward the old boardinghouse Aunt Win called an inn. Dee's whole face felt numb. She was sure her nose and ears were going to freeze off!

"It's a short ride," her aunt said, as if reading Dee's mind. She didn't seem the least bit bothered by the freezing winds. "You probably won't recognize the place."

"Probably not—since I don't remember it at all!" Dee shouted.

"Well, it's completely empty now, except for you and me. The last guests left right after Labor Day," Aunt Win said. She swerved suddenly, just missing a basset hound asleep in the road.

Then she looked over at Dee and smiled. "The inn is so old, and empty, and creaky, you'll probably think it's haunted. . . ."

CHAPTER
3

MISTY ISLAND INN. The wooden sign at the end of the gravel drive swayed and creaked in the wind. The old Victorian house, its shutters banging in welcome, looked as dark and desolate as Aunt Winnifred had described.

Dee's room at the end of the long, carpeted second floor hallway was bright and cozy, though. Aunt Win had hung gauzy white curtains at the windows and spread a bright red-and-yellow antique quilt on the four-poster bed.

Dee unpacked quickly, hanging her clothes in the deep closet that ran the length of the room and smelled strongly of mothballs. She tossed her Walkman onto the dresser. Beside it, she set down the copy of *Anne of Green Gables* she had just started reading.

A feeling of gloom settled over Dee despite her aunt's attempts to make her feel at home. How am I ever going to spend an entire winter in this creepy old place? she wondered. What will Aunt Win and I talk about? What will I do without any friends here?

Dee stood before the antique oval mirror above her dresser and absently combed her fingers through her short blonde hair. As she gazed at her reflection, her green eyes focused on the silver pendant and something seemed to catch in her throat. She could feel all of the summer's sadness returning, washing over her like waves on the beach.

She flopped onto the bed and the old mattress creaked under her weight. She put her hands up to her cheeks to try holding the tears back. Her hands were cold, and her face felt hot.

There was a sudden movement at the window, and Dee dropped her hands and looked up. The long, sheer curtains were swaying, as if someone had pushed them aside.

"Just the wind," she told herself. "Aunt Winnifred must've left the window open."

Dee climbed off the bed and crossed the room. To her surprise, the window was closed.

This place is awfully drafty, Dee thought as she turned off the lamp and went downstairs to dinner.

"My own special fish stew," Aunt Winnifred proclaimed, taking Dee's hand and pulling her to a table in the middle of the big kitchen.

"Mmmm, smells good," Dee said, forcing a smile. "What's in it?"

"Just about everything I could find," Aunt Winnifred said, plopping down on a seat across from Dee. "Is your room okay? I tried to brighten it up a bit for you. This inn gets so much wear and tear during the season. We were full up the entire summer. Hard to believe it now, huh? Now, we're full up with empty!" She laughed heartily at her own joke.

They both dug into the big, steaming bowls of stew. "Delicious," Dee said. "Real clams."

"One of the many advantages to living on an island like this," her aunt replied. "Hey—what's Dee short for, anyway? Delilah?"

The question caught Dee by surprise. She laughed. "It's short for Delightful!" she cracked. "Or maybe Demented."

"I believe it," Aunt Winnifred said.

"Seriously. It isn't short for anything. It's just Dee."

"What kind of name is that for a young woman?" Aunt Winnifred exclaimed. "What did your parents do—name you after a letter of the alphabet?"

"That's right," Dee told her. "They didn't like A, B, or C. So they decided on D."

"You're starting to make as much sense as I do," Aunt Winnifred said.

Aunt Winnifred kept up the lively conversation throughout dinner. She seemed to know exactly how to make Dee laugh.

After dinner, Dee found herself feeling unexpectedly warm and comfortable, and a lot less gloomy. Still, she was exhausted from the trip, so she kissed her aunt good night and climbed the creaking wooden steps that led to her room.

Dee stopped short at the doorway, suddenly feeling wide awake.

"I don't believe this!" she exclaimed.

Someone had been in her room.

Her denim skirt and green Shetland sweater had been neatly laid out on the bed.

"Who's in here?" Dee called.

Silence.

She stepped into the room. "Hey!" Her cassettes were spread across the dresser, and *Anne of Green Gables* was open beside them.

"Hey, if you're a thief and you're in the closet, I don't have anything worth stealing!" Dee called.

No reply.

She looked at the window. It was still closed. The intruder clearly hadn't come in that way.

Should she look in the closet? Or should she call her aunt?

Dee did both.

The floorboards squeaked as she tiptoed to the closet. Gathering all of her courage, she yanked open the door and grabbed at air until she found the light chain. Heart pounding, Dee gave it a tug. The closet light went on.

No one.

Seconds later, Winnifred came bounding up the stairs. "What is it, Dee? Is something wrong?"

"The inn isn't empty," Dee told her. "Look." She pointed to the skirt and sweater on her bed.

Aunt Winnifred looked confused. "Yes? Don't those belong to you?"

"Well, yes. But I didn't put them there," Dee said.

Aunt Win's expression changed from confusion to skepticism as Dee insisted that someone had moved her things around. "Maybe you're just not remembering correctly, dear. You had such a long, tiring trip. And I nearly turned you into an ice cube before I got you home. You probably moved them yourself."

"My *brain* wasn't frozen," Dee insisted. "Somebody's been in this room."

Winnifred walked over to the window and pushed the curtains out of the way. "The window is closed and locked," she said, looking out onto the grounds. "You have a beautiful dogwood tree right outside your window. Wait till you see it in the springtime when the white blossoms are all out. It's truly breathtaking. The nicest dogwood tree I've seen."

Aunt Win went on talking about dogwood trees for a few moments more, then said, "Good night, Dee. Sleep well. I'm sure you'll feel more at home tomorrow." And after giving her niece a warm, wet kiss on the forehead, she left the room.

Dee shrugged and started to undress. Maybe she'd get to the bottom of this mystery tomorrow. Maybe she wouldn't. But right now, she was too tired to worry about it.

She hung the denim skirt and green sweater back in the closet, pulled on a warm flannel nightgown, and climbed under the quilt.

The bed was hard and creaky, and no matter how she positioned herself, a mattress spring poked her in the back. Dee tossed and turned uncomfortably for nearly an hour.

A while later, Dee awoke with a start. Something soft had brushed against her face! She peered into the darkness and saw a pair of bright periwinkle blue eyes peering back. The eyes shimmered above her, seeming to float in midair.

A pale oval of a face. Someone was staring at her.

"Who is it? Who's there?" Fear tightened Dee's throat. She shivered beneath the quilt. "Who are you?"

Silence. And then the face seemed to dissolve in a gust of cold wind.

It's only a dream, Dee told herself. And, with that, she sank back onto the warm, goose-down pillow and slept fitfully for the rest of the night.

When Dee awoke the next morning, she found her blue running suit carefully laid out at the foot of her bed.

CHAPTER
4

Dee spent most of the morning walking around the grounds of the old inn, exploring the guest house in back, and swinging in the soft canvas hammock strung between two tall maple trees. The sun had come out, warming Misty Island and brightening Dee's outlook.

She spent the afternoon in the big kitchen, helping Aunt Winnifred chop pickles and peppers to make jar after jar of piccalilli—a spicy relish. "You can never have enough piccalilli," Aunt Win declared cheerfully, chopping away. "I'd certainly hate to run out."

"Yeah," Dee replied, barely hearing a word her aunt said.

Dee couldn't stop thinking about the mysterious goings-on in her bedroom. Every time she went up there, something had been moved.

She'd told Aunt Win about the running suit at breakfast. But again her aunt had dismissed Dee's fears, claiming that a bad memory was obviously an inherited trait.

Why won't she believe me? Dee asked herself, feeling frustrated and a little hurt. But then she thought, *Why* should *she believe me? There doesn't seem to be anyone else in the house, nothing at all has been stolen, and I don't have any real proof.*

So Dee decided to get some proof.

That night after dinner, she went up to her room. Sure enough, her Walkman had been moved from the dresser to the bed. And the closet door, which she had deliberately closed tight, was wide open.

"What's going on here?" she said aloud, feeling both frightened and excited.

Dee pulled on a crimson and gray Harvard sweatshirt, gave her hair a quick swipe with the brush, and walked to the doorway.

"Aunt Winnifred," she called loudly. "It's a beautiful night. I think I'll go for a long walk." Dee knew her aunt was in the cellar putting away the jars of piccalilli and couldn't hear her. The loud words were meant for the person or thing that was invading her room.

Leaving the lamp on, Dee closed the bedroom door behind her and clomped noisily through the long, dark hall, then down the creaking stairway. She walked out the front door, slamming it behind her.

The night was warm and clear, and the sky was full of twinkling stars. A soft, salty ocean breeze whispered through the trees.

Instead of following the winding flagstone walk to the bottom of the hill, Dee turned and marched quickly around to the side of the house. She had checked out the old dogwood tree earlier that afternoon. Its low, sturdy branches seemed perfect for climbing.

Still, Dee had to jump to reach the lowest branch, and she pulled herself up with some difficulty. A summer spent moping around the house instead of swimming on Cape Cod had definitely slowed her down.

The rest of the climb was pretty easy, though. The bark was soft and moist, and the tree supported her weight without bending. Dee climbed out onto a wide branch, pushing aside a dry clump of leaves. From there, she had a perfect view through her bedroom window. She could see the end of her bed, part of her dresser, and the open closet door.

Open? She could have sworn she'd closed it. Was someone in her room now?

Dee felt her heart begin to pound. She was only about four feet away from the house, but the window hadn't been cleaned in some time. A thin layer of dust gave an eerie, filmy quality to everything in the room. The wind picked up and the tree swayed. She gripped the branch with both hands and stared through the window.

A shadow crossed in front of the bed. Dee gasped. It wasn't a shadow. It was a girl.

The girl seemed to glide past the window to the closet.

Her heart pounding, Dee cautiously pulled herself forward on the branch. She had to get a closer look at the intruder.

But the girl seemed to fade away. Dee squinted hard. Suddenly the girl appeared again, right in front of the window. Dee saw that she had pale, pale skin and a small oval face framed by long auburn ringlets. She was wearing a puff-sleeved white blouse with a high collar under a long black pinafore.

What is she dressed up for—a part in Little Women? Dee asked herself. Staring in disbelief, she edged out even closer to the window.

The girl picked up Dee's Walkman and began fiddling with the buttons as if she wasn't quite sure how to work it. When the cassette holder popped open, she dropped the Walkman onto the bed in surprise.

"This is too much!" Dee muttered aloud. "Wait till Aunt Winnifred learns there's another girl hiding in the—"

What Dee saw next made her stop in midsentence. Her mouth dropped open, and she nearly lost her grip on the tree branch.

The girl vanished into thin air! Seconds later, just her head reappeared, floating above Dee's bed. The rest of her seemed to flicker back for a few seconds. Then she disappeared completely, and Dee's Walkman floated off the bed and hung suspended in the air.

Frozen with fear, Dee hugged the branch tighter. She had to hold on to something solid and real because what she was seeing was so totally unreal!

The girl in her bedroom wasn't a girl—she was a ghost!

CHAPTER
5

Dee started to edge back along the branch, feeling dizzy and weak. *I've got to get away,* she thought, panic-stricken. *I've got to tell Aunt Win!*

Dee had seen enough horror movies to know what the ghost wanted. She had already taken over Dee's belongings. Now she wanted to take over Dee's body. She wanted to *possess* Dee!

"I won't let her! I *won't!*" Dee muttered out loud, watching the Walkman float across the room toward the dresser, seeing the ghost girl's spooky white face glimmer and then fade.

What was that sound? Dee could hardly hear anything over the pounding of her heart and the rush of her thoughts.

It was a cracking sound.

The tree branch was breaking under her weight! She looked desperately for another branch. There was one just above her head. If only . . . but no. She couldn't reach it.

The cracking sound grew louder. Closer. The branch began to tilt.

Help! Dee tried to scream. But nothing came out.

The branch split with surprising suddenness. Dee felt it dropping away from her. I'm on air now, she thought. Just air.

As she started to fall, Dee threw up her arms and made a frantic grab for the window ledge. She caught it. And then her body slammed against the side of the shingled house, the impact knocking the breath out of her.

Dee gasped for air, knowing she had to hold on. *Hold on. Hold on.* She repeated the words to herself until she began to breathe normally again. Now all she had to do was pull herself up.

But that wasn't nearly as easy as it sounded. Dee just wasn't strong enough. Her arms ached, and her hands started to slip off the narrow wood ledge.

"Help! H-e-e-e-l-p!" The words came out more a moan than a cry.

Suddenly, the bedroom window slid open.

The ghostly face peered down at Dee, eyes glowing like bright blue flames.

"No—please!" Dee cried, struggling to maintain her grip on the window ledge. "Leave me alone! Please! Leave me alone!"

CHAPTER
6

Two hands reached out and grabbed Dee's. The ghost's hands were surprisingly warm and strong—like *real* hands. The ghost girl tightened her grip. Her eyes opened wide.

"LET ME GO! PLEASE!" Dee pleaded, squirming and kicking her feet. She didn't want to fall. But she didn't want to be captured by a ghost, either!

As the ghost girl struggled to pull Dee up into the window, the effort showed on her face. With each tug, her features faded. She became nearly transparent, just the outline of a face, two shoulders, two arms.

A few seconds later Dee was hanging over

the window ledge, leaning into her bedroom. Each second had seemed like an hour.

The ghost gave one last, hard tug, and Dee slid into the room. She hit the floor hard, wincing at the shock of pain in her knees. The room tilted from side to side and began to blur. Then everything became clear again, clear and almost blindingly bright.

I'm alive, Dee thought. *I'm still alive. And I'm still me. She hasn't possessed me, yet.*

She climbed shakily to her feet. Where was the ghost?

Dee looked around the still tilting room. There—slumped on the bed was the dim outline of a girl. She was gasping for breath, too. And Dee could see right through her!

A cold chill ran down Dee's spine. She started to say something, but the words stuck in her throat. She realized she had her back pressed against the wall in her desire to get as far away from this creature as possible.

The two girls stared at each other. Neither one moved. Slowly, the ghost girl seemed to revive. First, her pale skin came back into view. Then her long jumper, a shadowy gray, darkened to black. The auburn curls filled in around the perfect oval of a face.

"You—you're real," Dee managed to say.

"Not as real as you," the ghost girl said. Her voice was soft and breathy, as if being carried a great distance on the wind. She continued to stare into Dee's eyes.

Dee looked away as an old saying flashed into her mind: "The eyes are the window to the soul."

Deliberately avoiding the ghostly gaze, Dee looked around the room for a weapon, something she could use when the ghost attacked her. The dresser lamp, maybe. No. It looked too heavy. There was an umbrella in the closet, she remembered. But what good would an umbrella be against a ghost?

What good would *anything* be against a ghost?

The ghost girl shifted her legs beneath the long jumper. Dee's heart leapt. Was she getting ready to stand up, to come after Dee?

Yes. She did stand up. She took a few steps forward. Her footsteps didn't make a sound. She seemed to float across the floor.

Dee tried to back up, but she was already against the wall. She decided to duck under the ghost when she attacked, and then run out of the room.

"I suppose I should introduce myself," the

ghost girl said suddenly, shyly dropping her eyes. The dark red ringlets fell around her face as she lowered her head.

She is kind of pretty, Dee thought. *If I ignore the old-fashioned hairstyle and clothing, she looks about my age.*

"My name is Louisa Lockwood," the ghost said. She gave a small, awkward curtsy and then came a few steps closer.

"And I'm the Ghost of Christmas Past," Dee cracked nervously.

The girl's blue eyes widened in surprise. "Have *you* read the works of Dickens?" she asked.

Dee prepared to run. The ghost was obviously trying to lull her into a false sense of security, Dee reasoned. First she would catch Dee off guard. Then she'd pounce!

"It's been so long since I discussed books with someone," Louisa went on. She bit her lower lip, then seemed to grow paler.

I'm not falling for this, Dee told herself. The ghost had already moved into her room and tampered with her things. What was she going to do next?

Dee was determined to find out. "What do

you want?" she cried out angrily. "Why have you been hanging around in my room?"

"Hanging?" Louisa gave her a puzzled look. "I have not been hanging."

"What do you want?" Dee repeated.

The angry words seemed to surprise the girl. She looked hurt. Turning away from Dee, she took a few silent steps and slumped back onto the bed.

"You must want something," Dee insisted. "What?"

"Just a friend, I guess," Louisa said in a whisper. "I was hoping that you . . ." Her voice trailed off, as wispy as the rest of her. The ghost girl suddenly looked very tiny and very sad. The light from the dresser seemed to shine right through her. Dee noticed that she left no shadow on the bed or wall.

Dee started to sit down on the floor, but stopped herself. She didn't want to get too comfortable. "Are you really a ghost?" she asked, leaning back against the wall.

"Yes," Louisa replied in a whisper. "It seems that I am."

"Wow!" Dee exclaimed.

"I do not know that word," Louisa said, wrinkling her forehead. "What does it mean?"

"Wow? It means . . . well . . . it just means wow. It's kind of dumb. So why have you been . . . uh . . . haunting my room?"

"This is *my* room," the ghost girl said, standing up quickly.

Dee tensed and stepped away from the wall, preparing to run if the ghost made any threatening move.

But Louisa turned toward the closet and began pacing back and forth on silent footsteps. "I mean it *was* my room," she told Dee. "This is where my house stood, before the—before the . . ." Dee didn't hear the last word. Once again, Louisa's soft voice faded to silence. Then she floated back onto the bed, her pale face flickering like a lightbulb about to go out.

"How old are you—I mean *were* you," Dee asked, "when you . . . when . . ."

"When I died?" Louisa supplied. "It's quite all right to say it." She shrugged. It was a gesture filled with sadness. "Thirteen."

"Me, too!" Dee cried. "That's how old I am!"

Louisa nodded. She rubbed her chalk-white hands through her hair. The ringlets bounced right back into place.

"Wow!" Dee repeated. "I mean, how awful. And this was your room?" Dee stared at the flickering figure of the girl on the bed. She looked so weak and pitiful. But maybe it was just a trick. Maybe the ghost was just waiting for the right moment to spring.

"Why did you rearrange my clothes and move my stuff around?" Dee asked suspiciously.

After a long pause, the ghost girl finally answered. "Forgive me," she said at last. "I just wanted to examine them. I've never seen—or touched—such marvelous things. But I didn't take anything." She bit her lower lip again. "I didn't mean to frighten you," she said. "I guess I can't help frightening people. That's about all I *can* do."

"And you don't plan to kill me?" Dee asked, starting to feel a bit braver, a bit more like herself.

"Of course not."

"And you don't want to inhabit my body?"

"What?"

"You know. Inhabit my body. Possess my soul."

Dee listened in amazement as the ghost girl giggled. It sounded like someone tapping their fingers around on the highest piano keys. "That sounds complicated," Louisa exclaimed, still giggling. "I don't think I would know how to do that!"

Dee laughed, too, more from relief than amusement.

At that moment, Aunt Win poked her head into the room, startling them both. "Dee, what's going on?" she asked.

Dee looked at the bed. Louisa had vanished without a trace. "What?"

"I thought I heard you talking to someone," Aunt Win said.

"Oh. No. No, I wasn't," Dee replied, thinking quickly. "That was my Walkman. I hooked it up to my little speakers. I was . . . uh . . . listening to one of those books, you know, on tape."

"I see," said Aunt Win. "But I was sure I heard *two* voices."

"Of course," Dee told her. "There are two speakers. It's in stereo!"

Aunt Win smiled, but she didn't look convinced.

CHAPTER
7

"Louisa," Dee whispered as soon as her aunt had gone back downstairs.

There was no reply.

Good, Dee thought. She's gone. Maybe Aunt Win frightened her away for good.

But that didn't make any sense. Dee realized she wasn't thinking clearly. Did she want Louisa to still be there? No. Well . . . yes. Did she believe her story? Well, yes. Maybe. Was she still frightened of the ghost girl? No. Well . . . yes.

Of course she was frightened. Dee remembered a scene from an old horror film. The ghost in that movie had seemed so sweet and quiet at first. But then she'd suddenly bared her teeth and turned into a hideous monster.

Dee decided she had to keep her guard up. Maybe Louisa was just posing as a thirteen-year-old girl so she could trick Dee and snatch away her soul—or whatever it was that ghosts snatched away.

Dee shivered. She realized that she was frightened, but she was also curious. She wanted to hear more. "Louisa?" she repeated, a little louder.

"Yes, I am here," the soft voice replied. "It always takes me a little while to make myself visible. It isn't as easy as it looks." Louisa's outline reappeared on the bed. The colors slowly began to fill in.

"You sure disappeared fast," Dee said uneasily.

"Yes, going away is a lot faster than coming back," Louisa agreed, looking quite solid again.

"Can anybody see you," Dee asked, "or just me?"

"When I'm visible, anybody can see me. And touch me. But I stay invisible most of the time. I feel more comfortable that way—much safer. Besides, I don't like scaring people." Her blue eyes seemed to be far away, as if she were staring off into the past.

"People are scared of ghosts, whether they're visible or invisible," Dee said sharply.

Louisa lowered her eyes, and Dee realized she'd hurt the ghost girl's feelings again. She quickly tried to change the subject. "You're so pretty," she said.

Louisa shook her head. "No. *You* are pretty," she said. "I've been watching you. I admire the way you wear your hair short like a boy."

"A boy?" Dee's blonde hair was short—but not that short! "Thanks for the compliment!" Dee laughed. She realized that she no longer felt afraid of Louisa. Instead, she found herself feeling terribly sorry for her. Dee didn't want to spend one winter on Misty Island. She couldn't imagine having to spend eternity here!

Dee shivered again. She had been concentrating so hard on Louisa, she hadn't noticed the gusting, cold wind blowing in through the open window. Now she turned and pushed the window down. The effort took all of her strength. The old wooden frame was warped, and the window didn't slide easily.

"I'm so cold," Dee said. "Okay if I get changed and slip under the covers?"

This is weird, Dee thought. *I'm asking a ghost for permission to climb into my own bed!*

Or *was* it her bed? Was it actually Louisa's bed? Was Dee the unwanted intruder?

"It is your room now. I guess I am just a . . . a visitor," Louisa said, standing up awkwardly and backing toward the doorway. "May I stay?" she added eagerly.

Dee felt another stab of pity for the ghost girl. The poor thing must be terribly lonely. "Of course," she said.

Louisa smiled happily.

Dee went into the big closet and changed into her flannel nightgown. Then she tiptoed over the cold, bare floor and leaped into bed, pulling the covers up to her chin.

Louisa was standing by the dresser, examining Dee's copy of *Anne of Green Gables*. "I keep admiring this book," Louisa said. "It's so shiny. The books I had were never so shiny. And they never had pictures right on the front."

"It's called a paperback," Dee told her. "Come over here. Come sit down. Aren't you cold?"

"I don't seem to get cold—or hot," Louisa said, putting down the book. "I am always the same." She floated over to the bed. "Is it all right if I sit here?" she asked, pointing to the bottom of the bed.

Uh-oh, that's a little close, Dee thought. But Louisa looked so frail and uncomfortable, Dee was once more reassured. "Sure. Come on. Get comfortable," she said.

As the ghost girl settled onto the foot of the bed and tucked her thin legs under her wide skirt, Dee got a glimpse of her shoes. They were very narrow, and black, and had a row of buttons going up the front instead of laces.

The old radiator against the wall suddenly chugged to life. It began rattling loudly, and wisps of steam darted out from underneath it.

Dee smiled. Soon it would be toasty warm in the room. "Have you always lived on Misty Island?" she asked.

Louisa sighed. "Always. I was born in 1884 right on this spot. I mean, our house was right on this spot."

"So it must have been—" Dee stopped for a minute to figure it out— "1897 when you . . . died." She still had trouble saying the word, but Louisa didn't seem to mind.

"Gosh, I've never asked this question of anyone," Dee went on. "But how did you, uh, die? Did it hurt?"

"No. I don't recall any pain," Louisa said, closing her eyes as if trying to see it happening again. "There was a terrible fire. I was asleep. Our house went up in flames. I didn't see it. We were all asleep. I guess it happened very quickly. My whole family died—me, my parents, my little brother, Edward. Everyone."

"Wow," Dee said. "What did it feel like to be dead?" Then, when she saw that Louisa's eyes had filled with tears, she quickly added, "Oh, I'm sorry!"

"No. It's all right," Louisa said, rubbing the tears away. "I honestly don't mind talking about it. I really want to tell you. But sometimes when I think of my family—" Her voice cracked as fresh tears ran slowly down her pale cheeks. "I miss them *so much!*" she sobbed.

Dee climbed out of bed and brought Louisa some tissues from her dresser. She tenderly put a hand on the ghost's shoulder and waited for her to stop crying.

Dee couldn't believe she had been terrified of Louisa just a few minutes before. *What a terrible life she has,* Dee thought. *And she isn't even alive!*

Dee's hand automatically reached for the silver dove pendant around her neck. She pictured her mother's face, her golden blonde hair blowing in the wind. The memory made her feel even closer to Louisa.

After a while, Louisa became calm again. "Where was I?" she asked, settling down on the edge of the bed. Her skin was nearly as white as the high-necked blouse she wore, but her eyes were dark blue and shining.

"You were telling me about the fire," Dee said. "How you died in your sleep. Do you remember what it felt like, how it felt to be dead?"

"I don't remember the early part very well," Louisa said, "only the smell of the smoke and the sound of the flames. And then I was walking with my family. We were walking for a long, long time, but we didn't get tired.

"My mother was holding my hand. She seemed quite calm and peaceful. I felt calm and peaceful, too. No. I guess I felt nothing at all. Empty. Just empty.

"We walked and walked. Then suddenly I let go of my mother's hand. I turned back. I'm not really certain why. I just wanted to see everything one last time. I wanted to see our house, everything we were leaving behind.

"It was only for a second, but when I turned

around again, my family was gone. I was all alone in the darkness. I called to them, but there was no reply. I ran after them, but they'd vanished completely. I didn't know what to do then, so I started running back to our house.

"Getting back seemed to take forever. When I got there, the house was still burning. It was the most horrifying thing I'd ever seen. But I couldn't take my eyes off it. I sat down on a rock and watched the flames shoot out of the windows. When the roof fell in, the ground seemed to shake. The house burned all night, and I sat there watching it."

"How dreadful," Dee said softly.

"I didn't realize how dreadful it was until the fire was put out. I sat there staring at the smoking pieces of wood, all that was left of my house, of my family. My house was gone. Everything was gone. I was all alone—not with the living, not with the dead.

"The morning was early, still gray. A light rain was falling, but I couldn't feel it. After a while, I fell asleep. And then . . ."

"Then what happened?" Dee asked impatiently.

"Then I woke up in this room! A strange woman—your Aunt Winnifred—was running a loud machine of some sort over the floor. It was gobbling up all the fluff from under the bed."

"A vacuum cleaner."

"I was very confused," Louisa said, playing with the end of the quilt. "I didn't know where I was. I didn't know who the woman was. I was terrified of the loud machine. Your aunt was busy fixing up the room. After she finished with the machine, she started to put up curtains. I was so confused, I thought she was preparing the room for *me*."

"How awful," Dee said softly.

"I went over to thank her and to introduce myself," Louisa continued. "But she couldn't see me. That's when I remembered I was dead. My house was gone, but your aunt's house had been built on its ashes. So, in a way, this really *was* my room!"

"So what did you do?" Dee asked, sitting up.

"I couldn't decide what to do. I wandered all around the house. I walked and then I floated. Suddenly, I saw my hand. I had made myself visible. I stayed in this room for hours, practicing, making myself appear and then disappear. I looked at things. I touched things. I found a calendar in your aunt's kitchen. When I saw the year on it, I could hardly believe my eyes.

"I realized that I had been asleep for nearly a hundred years. I was very upset and very frightened. So I came back here. This room was so pretty and cheerful-looking that I decided to stay.

"That night I had a dream—at least, I think it was a dream—in which my mother came to me. She looked very beautiful but very troubled. I was so glad to see her, I reached out to her. I wanted to touch her, but I couldn't. An invisible wall seemed to stand between us.

"She explained that I was a lost soul, trapped between the land of the living and the land of the dead. I told her how much I missed her and my father and my little brother. 'Tell me how to get back to you,' I cried.

"She told me she'd heard it might be possible, but that it wouldn't be easy. She told me that I would first have to change the lives of four people who were related to me, to make their lives better. Only then would I no longer be a lost soul. Only then would I be allowed to rejoin my family.

" 'Try, Louisa,' my mother pleaded. 'I'm waiting for you, honey. You have only one year to help the four relatives. So please try. We all want to have you back with us again.'

"Those were her last words to me," Louisa said. Her voice was so low Dee had to lean forward to hear her. "And the very next day, Dee, *you* arrived. At first I was miserable that the room would no longer be mine. But when I saw that you were about my age, I felt a little better. I thought maybe I could talk to you, maybe you would keep me from feeling so lonely, maybe . . ."

Dee started to speak, but she didn't know quite what to say. "I lost someone this summer," she said finally, the words catching in her throat. But after hearing Louisa's painful story, Dee felt uncomfortable talking about herself.

The two girls sat in silence for a long while, listening to the gentle hissing of the radiator, not looking at each other. Finally Dee broke the silence. "Listen, I'm going to be here all winter," she said. "I'll help you find your four relatives, Louisa. I'll help you help them."

Louisa let out a soft sigh. "I thank you for your kind offer," she said politely. "But I don't see how you can. I'm afraid I don't even *have* four relatives."

CHAPTER
8

The next morning, Dee was awakened by the bright sunlight pouring through her bedroom window. She pulled herself up slowly, rubbing her eyes. She hadn't slept well. Strange dreams, dreams in which she was a little girl back home in Cambridge, had interrupted her sleep.

Now as she awoke, she didn't remember the dreams. She only remembered the feeling of sadness they had brought her.

She lowered her feet to the floor and stretched sleepily. The floorboards were cold. She wrapped her flannel robe around her and thought about curling back under the warm quilt.

But then she remembered Louisa and was jolted awake. Louisa! Had she been a dream, too? With the morning sun flooding the room and the sweet aroma of pancakes on the griddle drifting up from the kitchen, Louisa and her sad, mysterious story seemed as unreal as Dee's dreams.

"Louisa?" Dee whispered.

No reply. Where was she? Had she fallen asleep and gone back to that limbo where she'd spent the last hundred years?

"Louisa!" Dee called, a little louder.

Still no reply.

Dee climbed out of bed, hopped over the cold floor to the closet, and pulled out a pair of faded jeans and a sweatshirt. For some reason, Louisa's silence made Dee feel frightened again.

This house is haunted! Dee thought. But what if Louisa isn't the only ghost? What if there are others lurking here, and they just used Louisa to make me feel safe, to make me think they mean no harm? What if there is no Louisa, never was a Louisa?

"Why am I having these strange thoughts?" Dee asked herself, as she laced her sneakers. "Maybe the ghost has already started to take over my mind!"

46

Dee ran out of the room, down the old staircase, two steps at a time, and into the kitchen. Aunt Win was standing over the griddle, tending the pancakes with a long-handled spatula.

"Aunt Win, this house is haunted!" Dee burst in.

Her aunt didn't turn around. She chuckled. "Probably," she said calmly.

"No—really!"

Aunt Win flipped a very large, perfectly round pancake before she finally turned to Dee. "Most of the old houses on Misty Island are haunted, I think. That's what gives them their charm."

"But, Aunt Win—"

"This old inn is so empty, we could use a ghost or two to liven it up." She piled a big stack of pancakes onto a plate and handed it·to Dee. "You look tired, dear. Didn't you sleep well? Maybe we should try a different mattress. The one in Room 3B is fairly new."

"No, Aunt Win, the mattress is fine," Dee said, nearly dropping the plate of pancakes. "I never sleep well in a new place." Dee decided to change the subject. She didn't want her aunt to think she was crazy. "This is a huge stack of pancakes. Are we expecting company for breakfast?"

"Those are for you. I already ate," Aunt Win said, scraping the griddle. "I can make more if you like."

"No. These should last me the whole winter!" Dee exclaimed, reaching for the syrup. They both laughed.

Aunt Win pulled up a chair and sat down across from Dee. "I have an Historical Society luncheon today. I have to leave in a few minutes. I'm afraid I won't be able to entertain you this morning."

"That's okay," Dee said, trying to talk around a mouthful of pancakes. "I got used to being alone . . . during the summer. I mean . . ."

"I guess it'll be pretty lonely for you here till school starts," Aunt Win said wistfully. "But that's only a couple of weeks away."

"Don't worry," Dee said, wiping syrup off her chin. "I'll be fine." But then she thought of Louisa, and she wasn't so sure. She decided she'd better get away, out of the house. She didn't want to be there all alone with a ghost. "I think I'll take a walk, do some exploring."

"Good idea," Aunt Win said, before getting up to leave. "It's a beautiful day."

Dee surprised herself by eating almost all of the pancakes on her plate. Then she went back to her room and brushed her hair. Still no sign of Louisa. Dee was glad. She hurried down the stairs and was almost at the front door when the phone rang.

Dee ran back to the kitchen and snatched the receiver up in the middle of a ring. "Daddy? Oh, hi." Her father sounded so far away. It was a very bad connection. "Fine. Yes. Just fine. Yeah. Mr. Spalding was waiting with the ferry. Right. Aunt Win? She's terrific. Yes. Yes. I'm just getting settled in, and I'm fine."

She considered telling her father about Louisa. But what could he do from so far away? And why should she trouble him? He sounded so sad. He kept repeating how he missed her already. His voice was so faint and so far away, he sounded like a ghost himself.

"Okay, Daddy, I will. Yes. I'll tell her. Call again soon, okay? Okay? Yes. I love you, too. 'Bye."

When she hung up the phone, Dee had tears in her eyes. How could her father have done this to her? she wondered. Weren't families supposed to stay together? And why had his call made her feel so awful? She tried not to think about it. Instead she pulled a windbreaker from the hall closet and ran outside.

The day was crisp, and the cool, moist air felt good on Dee's face. She took a deep breath. Even though Aunt Win's inn was a bit of a walk from the shore, Dee could still smell the salt on the wind. She watched two squirrels scampering between the trees that dotted the long, sloping lawn, then she headed down the flagstone path that led to the road.

Dee kicked at the fallen leaves as she walked. The trees were nearly bare. Fat, brown maple leaves blanketed the ground.

Walking quickly, Dee followed the macadam road that curved away from the inn. She started to jog.

A large, white Victorian house came into view. A blond-haired boy of seven or eight was bouncing a rubber ball against the side of the house. He stopped when he saw her and called to her. "Wanna play catch?"

"Not right now," Dee called back without slowing her pace. "Maybe later, okay?"

His shoulders drooped. He went back to bouncing the ball off the house. The poor kid must be lonely, too, Dee thought, and she decided she'd come back and play with him later. Maybe his parents would like her to baby-sit sometime.

The road curved again, and Dee followed it past a small grove of pine trees. She slowed her pace. She was breathing hard already!

On the other side of the woods stood a small graveyard on a low hill. Dee climbed the hill and followed the path of a large, white moth as it fluttered over the tombstones. She noticed that the stones looked very old. Many of them were worn and broken and tipped at odd angles. She pulled herself up and walked nearer, squinting to make out the dates on the old slate and granite markers.

They were all from the 1800's. Two tiny stones that stood side by side caught her eye. They each had the name CAWBER etched into them. Dee bent down to read the dates: 1890–1893. Two little Cawber children, both dead at the age of three.

Dee stood as a cold shiver ran down her back. They would have been alive when Louisa was alive. Louisa might have even known them . . . if there was a Louisa. If the ghost had been telling Dee the truth . . .

A large, white cloud drifted over the sun and the air suddenly grew colder.

What was that whisper?

Just the wind through the trees, Dee hoped with a shudder. So many dead souls beneath her feet. . . .

Dee scolded herself for feeling so afraid, then she decided to leave anyway. She started back down to the road, but another tombstone caught her eye. This one was tall, slender, and jutted up at an angle over the silky brown weeds. The name LOCKWOOD was cut deeply into the stone. Dee hurried over to read the rest of it.

THADDEUS LOCKWOOD. Dee ran her finger over the dates below, trying to make them out. The first date had been worn away by the years. But with some effort, she made out the second date—1897.

Wasn't that the year Louisa claimed her family had died? Dee thought so, but she couldn't remember.

The gravestone beside it had fallen down. Dee had to lean over it to make out the words: LAVINIA LOCKWOOD, 1866–1897. That had to be Louisa's mother, Dee thought, pushing a clump of tall grass aside to see if anything else was etched into the stone. There was nothing more.

She stood up slowly. Without realizing it, her hand had gone to the silver dove pendant around her neck. She saw her mother for an instant; she smiled then looked away. Dee forced the picture from her mind.

She moved over to the next gravestone, a smaller one with a long crack from top to bottom. "No!" Dee cried aloud as she read the name at the top.

LOUISA LOCKWOOD.

The dates on this stone were easy to read: 1884–1897.

Thirteen years. Just thirteen years.

Dee knew that if she kept looking she'd find another, even smaller stone—Louisa's brother Edward's. But she didn't have the heart for it.

Dee felt like crying, and then she *was* crying, and she didn't try to stop. She sobbed loudly and watched her tears drip onto the old tombstone, onto Louisa's tombstone.

And she knew that the poor, sad ghost girl had told her the truth.

"I'm going to help you, Louisa," Dee said, wiping the tears that ran down her cheeks. "I'm going to help you get back to your family, back where you belong."

CHAPTER
9

"Louisa, I found a relative—a Lockwood!"

Dee burst into her bedroom, holding the phone book. "Louisa? Where are you?"

There was a loud crash from the closet and Dee dropped the book. "Louisa? Is that you?"

The closet door opened slowly, and Louisa glided out, looking sheepish. "I'm very sorry. I accidentally knocked some packages off the shelf."

"You scared me to death!" Dee said, then blushed as she realized that wasn't the best expression to use around Louisa. "What were you doing in there? Where were you this morning? I called to you when I woke up."

55

"Sorry. I'm a very deep sleeper," Louisa said. "When I awoke, the house was empty. I . . . I was just admiring your garments." Louisa looked very guilty. "Look." She pulled her long, black skirt up a couple of inches to reveal a pair of Dee's pink high-top sneakers.

"Your shoes are so wonderful!" Louisa exclaimed. "They're so soft, and they have colors on them, and they don't have all those buttons to button." She took a few awkward steps into the middle of the room and tripped. She fell over the high wooden bedpost, and the bedpost appeared to go right through her chest and come out her back!

"Louisa!" Dee cried out in alarm. But it was clear the ghost girl wasn't the least bit hurt. "What *are* those things under your dress? Slips?" Dee asked as Louisa nonchalantly floated away from the bed.

"Do you mean my petticoats? You don't wear any petticoats, do you?"

"I wouldn't know one if I sat on one," Dee said, shaking her head.

"Here." Before Dee could protest, Louisa had slid the long white petticoats off and was offering them to her.

"Huh? No, really, I couldn't," Dee protested.

"Well. Okay." She took them from Louisa and then stopped. "Which is the front and which is the back?"

Louisa laughed. "Don't people know how to get dressed anymore?"

Dee pulled them up over her jeans. "These look really beautiful," she said, admiring herself in the mirror. "But they don't feel very good. They're so stiff."

"Of course," Louisa said. "They're starched."

Dee whirled around giddily, then slipped the petticoat off. "It looks better on you," she sighed. "I guess I'm more the sporty type."

Then, pulling Louisa to the closet, she said, "Here, now you try on some of *my* things. Let's see how you look."

"Can I really?" Louisa immediately became very excited. "Your clothes are like something in a dream. So soft. And so many colors. I didn't know there *were* so many colors!"

"Try these." Dee tossed Louisa a pair of jeans.

"Trousers? Oh no, I couldn't!" Louisa's mouth formed a little o of horror.

"Go ahead," Dee urged.

"Never!" Louisa insisted. "You look very nice dressing as a boy. But I couldn't do it."

Dee smiled. "Okay, no jeans. Here, try this." She tossed her a short plaid skirt.

Louisa held it up and examined it. "No, please! I could never wear this. My knees would show!"

"So what?" Dee cried.

"It isn't proper," Louisa said, running her hands over the soft cotton fabric.

"But you're usually invisible anyway!" Dee cried. "So who cares?"

"I care," Louisa said firmly.

Dee felt terrible. Why did she always have to shoot off her big mouth?

"Oh my goodness. Look at this color," Louisa exclaimed, pulling a bright red wool sweater off the shelf.

"Do you like it?" Dee asked, glad that Louisa had finally found something acceptable.

"It's sinful," Louisa said, rubbing the soft wool sleeve against her cheek.

"Does that mean you like it?"

Louisa looked shocked. "No! I said it was sinful. A respectable woman could not wear this."

Dee couldn't help it. She laughed. "Times have changed, Louisa," she said softly. "You can wear any color you like now."

"Do you mean it?" Louisa looked doubtful.

"Yes, I mean it. Go put on the sweater." She pulled Louisa away from the closet. Louisa stood in the middle of the room, trying to work up the courage to try on the red sweater.

Suddenly, the door swung open and Aunt Win appeared on the threshold. Instantly, Louisa tossed the sweater to Dee and vanished.

"Dee!" Aunt Win cried, quite alarmed. "That sweater—it seemed to float right into your hands!"

"Oh . . . uh . . . yes, I know," Dee replied. "I was just—" But before she could think up a logical explanation, Aunt Win got a good look at the room and cried, "Dee, your clothes. Why are they scattered about like that?"

"Oh. I was . . . just trying a few things on, seeing if they fit," Dee told her.

"A few?" Aunt Win said, smiling indulgently. And as Dee quickly began to straighten up the mess, her aunt said, "I came up here for a reason. I'm going to town to do some shopping tomorrow morning. I thought you might need some new clothes for school. But I guess you have enough." She shook her head in amusement before adding, "Still, you haven't seen our little town, yet. Maybe you'd like to come with me anyway, just for the ride."

"Well . . . sure," Dee said hesitantly. She'd been planning to help Louisa find her relative, the Lockwood Dee had found in the telephone book. But she didn't want to hurt her aunt's feelings. "That sounds great."

"It isn't great. But it's the only town we've got," Aunt Win said, heading out the bedroom door.

As soon as she was gone, Louisa slowly came back into view. "Dee, can I go to town with you?" she asked eagerly.

"What?"

"It's been nearly a hundred years," Louisa said. "I would love to see if anything has changed."

Dee laughed. "Of course you can come."

"Oh, thank you!" Louisa exclaimed, leaping up to the ceiling in her happiness. And she stayed there, floating beside the light fixture.

"Louisa, come down," Dee called up to her. "No. Don't come down. Teach *me* to do that! I want to come *up*!"

"I wish I could," Louisa said seriously. "But to be perfectly honest, I'm not quite sure how I do it myself."

Both girls suddenly started to giggle. Soon they were laughing uncontrollably like two old friends.

Helping Louisa was going to be fun, Dee realized. And it certainly wasn't going to be boring!

CHAPTER
10

"Here we are in town," Aunt Win announced, slowing the jeep. "Don't sneeze or you'll miss it."

"It's pretty," Dee said.

Actually, the town was just about what she'd expected. A white clapboard church, its pointed steeple recently painted, was set back from the road on a wide, leaf-covered lawn. The shops began on the next block. They were housed in low, two-story buildings—stores on the ground floor, living quarters above.

Most of the shops were closed and boarded up for winter. A small restaurant, The Misty Island Cafe & Clam Bar, was open. Next to it stood the post office, a flag above the doorway slapping loudly against the shingles as the wind gusted. Then came a few boarded-up shops, a general store, a fish store, a small supermarket, and a tiny barbershop. Through the window, Dee could see the barber sitting in his tall, black barber chair, reading a magazine.

Dee looked across the street. On the corner was a combination gas station and grocery store. A sign in the window said OPEN, but no one was there. Then came a narrow, empty lot; an ice cream parlor, boarded up; a clothing store, boarded up; and a small coffee shop called The Seafarer Inn.

A woman came out of the supermarket, plopped two large bags on the hood of her car, and waved to Aunt Win as she searched for her keys. At the same time, a tall, thin, shabbily dressed man carrying two torn brown shopping bags stepped slowly out of the small vacant lot. He stopped short when he saw Dee and Aunt Win drive past.

"Who is that?" Dee asked, startled by the man's ragged appearance.

"It's Mrs. O'Brien," Aunt Win said. "Look at her. Always losing her car keys. They're probably still in the ignition."

"No. The man," Dee said.

"Man?" Aunt Win looked in her rearview mirror. But there was no one to see. The man had disappeared. Pulling the jeep up to the curb in front of the fish store, she said, "Looks like a ghost town today."

That made Dee laugh. If Aunt Win only knew that she was sitting inches away from a real ghost!

Louisa reached over from the back seat and squeezed Dee's shoulder to make her stop laughing. "Ouch!" Dee cried.

"What's the matter?" Aunt Win asked, alarmed.

"Huh? Oh, nothing," Dee replied. "Something just stung me. Must have been a mosquito. I guess no one's told *them* that the season is over!"

It was her aunt's turn to laugh. "Spoken like a true islander." She ruffled Dee's hair, then climbed down quickly and closed the jeep door. Once again, Dee was surprised by her aunt's agility and speed.

"Why don't you go to the fish store, while I'm in the market," Aunt Win said. "See if they have any lobsters. I'll make my special chowder tonight, and we'll have a feast."

"Okay. Sounds good to me," Dee told her,

turning toward the window of the little fish store. A cardboard sign tilted against the glass advertised SPECIAL TODAY, but there was nothing written underneath.

"Don't get anything bigger than a pound and a half," Aunt Win called before disappearing into the market next door. "Bigger than that, they tend to get tough."

Dee stopped at the door to the fish store and said, "Louisa, are you here?"

"Yes, I am," Louisa's hesitant voice was right behind Dee. "The town certainly has grown since I was here last."

"Grown? What was it like then—two orange crates and a fire hydrant?" Dee teased.

"Fire hydrant? What is that?"

"Never mind," Dee said, shaking her head. "Let's go inside."

She pulled open the door, causing a bell attached to the doorknob to ring, and stepped inside. It was a brightly lit room with creaking wood floors and a single display case that ran the width of the store. A tray of fish sat on top of the case. Dee found herself staring into the glassy, blue eyes of a dozen pale flounders. She tore her gaze away from them. Seeing no one behind the counter, she called out, "Anyone here?"

"Be right with you," came a boy's voice from a room behind the display case.

Dee made a face for Louisa's benefit. "It stinks in here."

"I always loved the aroma of fish," Louisa replied wistfully. "It is a treat I haven't experienced in a long, long time. I loved the feel of fish, too. I used to clean them for my father." Suddenly, one of the fish on the tray floated up into the air. Dee realized that Louisa must have picked it up.

"Louisa—stop that! Put it down!" she whispered excitedly.

The fish plopped back onto the tray just as the boy came out from the back room.

"Hi," he said, giving Dee a shy smile.

He's kind of cute, Dee thought. The boy was about fourteen or fifteen, with a mop of curly brown hair, lively brown eyes, and an adorable smile.

"Hi," she said.

"Hi," he repeated, wiping his hands on the long, white apron he wore. He stared at her. "Do you live around here?"

"Well, not really," Dee said. "I mean, I'm

living here now. For awhile. I came to stay with my aunt Win."

"At the inn, right? I thought you were new," he said. "I mean—" he straightened the apron awkwardly—"I know just about everyone on Misty Island."

"He looks just like Tobias Dodge, a boy I liked!" Louisa whispered in Dee's ear. "How is that possible?"

"What?" Dee asked.

"I said I know just about everyone on the island," the boy said. "My name is Nicky Dodge."

"I'm Dee Forest. I'll bet your family's been on Misty Island for a long, long time," Dee said for Louisa's benefit. "Didn't you have a grandfather or great-grandfather named Tobias Dodge?"

"Probably," Nicky said, leaning forward over the glass counter. "A lot of the men in my family were named Tobias. How did you know?"

"Oh . . . my aunt's been telling me about the families who live here. Do you have any lobsters today?"

"Yeah. In back." He stared at her for a long time without taking a breath. "It must be kind of hard being new here," he said finally. "I mean, coming after the season and all."

"It's been kind of exciting, actually," Dee replied honestly.

"Well, there isn't much going on here in the fall. But would you like to go for a walk or something sometime?" Nicky asked.

He really *is* cute, Dee thought. "I don't know," she told him, staring into the display case. "I'm not going to be here that long really. Just a few months, you know, and then—"

The door swung open, letting in a blast of cool air. Dee turned around to see a young man of twenty-five or so, wearing a dark fur coat, rush into the store. Dee glanced at his face, then moved her eyes down to the coat. It was the most luxurious, beautiful fur coat she'd ever seen—especially on a man!

"You still here? Where's your father?" the man snapped at Nicky, his face tight with displeasure.

"He's still not feeling well, sir," Nicky said, backing away from the counter and standing up straight, almost as if at military attention.

"Is my mother's order ready?"

"I think so. Almost. I'll have to check," Nicky stammered.

"Well, why don't you just go and do that," the man said irritably.

Nicky obediently hurried into the back room.

The man glared at Dee, then turned his back on her. He had small, dark eyes, a short snub of a nose, and sandy-colored hair, slicked straight back. He really was very unpleasant-looking, Dee decided.

Nicky returned a few seconds later. "I'm sorry. That order isn't quite ready," he said.

"Can't you do *anything* right?" the man complained loudly. "I want to speak to your father."

"You can't. I told you. He's sick," Nicky said, looking very upset. "I'll put the order together right away, sir. And . . . I'll deliver it to your mother's myself at no extra charge."

"You'd better not be late with it," the man said. He swung around, bumping Dee with the sleeve of his big coat, then he marched out of the store. The door slammed hard behind him.

"What's *his* problem?" Dee asked, watching through the window as the man climbed into a bright green Jaguar and roared away.

"Him? He has no problems," Nicky muttered. "He only *makes* problems for other people."

"Who is he?" Dee asked.

"He's a creep. His name is Harry Lockwood."

"Lockwood?" Dee was nearly too startled to speak. "He's a Lockwood?"

"Yeah. Hard to believe, isn't it? His mother is so nice. You know her?"

"No. Not really," Dee replied. "I've just heard about her."

"Poor woman," Nicky said, shaking his head.

"Why? Because she has a mean son?"

"No. Because . . . Well, I shouldn't be gossiping. You're new here. You don't want to hear about it."

"No. I'm very interested. Really," Dee insisted. "What about Harry Lockwood?"

"Nothing," Nicky said, suddenly embarrassed. "But . . . well . . . you saw that coat he was wearing. And the car. Pretty fancy, huh? But Harry's never worked a day in his life."

"So how did he pay for all that?"

"No one knows," Nicky said, looking uncomfortable. "Hey, I'd better get Mrs. Lockwood's order together before he comes back. What can I get for you, Dee?"

"Oh. I almost forgot," Dee said. "Lobsters. Two lobsters. A pound and a half each, please."

A few seconds later, Nicky dropped two live

lobsters into a large plastic bag, tied it up, and handed it to Dee. She paid him quickly and turned to leave. She couldn't wait to get out of the store and talk to Louisa alone.

"Uh . . . see you sometime?" Nicky asked.

"Sure. Okay," Dee said. "Nice meeting you, Nicky."

Back on the deserted street, she called to Louisa. "Where are you? Did you hear what he said about that guy?"

"Yes, I heard," Louisa said, right next to her.

"Well? Don't you see what this means, Louisa? There are at least two Lockwoods on Misty Island. That means two relatives for you to help."

"Harry Lockwood doesn't look as if he needs much help," Louisa said.

"I think you're wrong," Dee said, waving to Aunt Win, who was coming down the street carrying two bags of groceries. "There's something about Harry that Nicky didn't want to tell us. But forget about him for now. As soon as we get home, we're going to go pay a visit to his mother!"

CHAPTER
11

After lunch, Dee and Louisa walked down the road to Mrs. Lockwood's house. Dee took a deep breath as she came to a field of long, pale grass bent low in the wind. The air smelled of fresh air and pine.

Dee hopped over a large puddle, the water shimmering in the sunlight. Louisa's feet seemed to float over the pavement, never making a sound. And when she hopped over the puddle, she made no reflection in the water.

She's a ghost, Dee thought. *I'm walking down the street with a ghost.* Dee suddenly felt afraid all over again.

But Dee's fear quickly gave way to pity. Poor Louisa, she thought. She probably couldn't feel the warmth of the sun or smell the sweetness of the air. How eerie not to see your shadow as you walk or hear your footsteps scrape along the road. How depressing to go through the New England fall without the taste of cold apple cider or steaming hot clam chowder.

I've got to help her, Dee thought. *She's the only friend I have on this island. But she doesn't belong here with me. She belongs with her family.*

If only Louisa could find a way to help Mrs. Lockwood and do a good deed to improve her relative's life. That would be one down and three to go. Helping four relatives shouldn't be that hard, should it? Dee wondered. Not if they worked together.

"Louisa," Dee said softly, "when we get to Mrs. Lockwood's, make yourself invisible and see what you can see. Get all the information you can."

"Information about what?"

"About anything! Look for ways we can help her. Check out all the rooms. See if anyone else lives there. The house might be crawling with relatives."

"Crawling? Do you mean babies?"

"Never mind," Dee said, chuckling. She kept forgetting that to Louisa, she practically spoke a foreign language! "I'll try to keep Mrs. Lockwood busy so you can dig around, okay?"

"Dig?"

The road curved to the left, revealing a majestic old three-story house of weathered gray shingles and navy blue shutters—the Lockwood house. Several relatively new wings had been added on either side of the original, box-style Colonial building, so that it now sprawled across the lawn.

"It's so big!" Louisa cried.

"It's a lovely old house," Dee replied.

"It was much smaller in my day. But it was nice even then," Louisa said.

The girls followed the curve of the narrow road to a white picket fence that separated the yard from the street. "What are you going to say to her?" Louisa asked, sounding worried.

"Oh, I don't know. I'll think of something," Dee answered casually, straightening her down vest and then smoothing her blonde hair with both hands. "In case you haven't noticed, I'm seldom at a loss for words."

Louisa started to laugh, but her laughter was cut short. "Who's that?" she cried, and vanished instantly.

A tall, thin man was leaning against the white

entrance gate. He jumped back guiltily when he spotted Dee.

Dee recognized him. He was the ragged-looking man she had seen in town that morning. Close up, he looked even shabbier now.

It was too late to turn back. As Dee slowly approached the gate, the man just as slowly backed away. Dee saw that his brown suit, an outdated single-breasted suit at least a size too big for him, was spotted and frayed. His trouser cuffs were caked with sand. His hair, all gray except or a few sandy-colored streaks, needed cutting. And he clearly hadn't shaved for days.

Dee froze. What did he want? Why was he hanging around Mrs. Lockwood's gate?

The man's eyes grew wide above his thin stubble of beard. He gave Dee a piercing stare. And then, without a word, he turned and ran.

The gate, which he must have opened, banged noisily against the fence. Dee watched until he disappeared around the bend in the road.

"Who was that man?" Louisa said, remaining invisible. "He looks awfully familiar."

"That's because we saw him in town this morning," Dee said.

"No," Louisa insisted. "That isn't it. I'm sure I've seen him somewhere else."

"Well, I wonder what he was doing here. Do you think he knows Mrs. Lockwood?"

"I doubt it," Louisa said. "He didn't look like he was paying a social call."

"Maybe we helped Mrs. Lockwood already by getting rid of that guy," Dee suggested.

"That would be wonderful," Louisa whispered, as Dee pushed open the gate. "But somehow I don't imagine it's going to be quite that simple. . . ."

CHAPTER

12

Dee lifted the brass knocker on the big oak front door, then jumped nervously at the sound of the loud clang.

"Maybe she isn't home," Louisa said, still invisible at Dee's side.

"You have a bad attitude," Dee scolded. "Of course she's home. Think positive."

Dee knocked again, harder. She stared at a small tear in the wire mesh of the screen door and waited.

A few seconds later, the door was pulled open a few inches. A tiny woman with large dark eyes and wavy brown hair peeked through the crack. "I thought I heard someone," she said. "I hope I didn't keep you waiting long. I was back in my greenhouse."

"Mrs. Lockwood?" Dee asked, a little surprised. She had expected someone older-looking. Mrs. Lockwood was not young. But with her lively eyes, delicate features, and high cheekbones, she was definitely a very attractive woman.

"Yes, that's me." Her voice also sounded surprisingly young to Dee.

"I'm Dee Forest. I'm new on Misty Island. I'm staying with my Aunt Winnifred. I wonder if I could talk to you for a few minutes."

Mrs. Lockwood pulled the door open a bit wider. She was wearing a calf-length, beige tweed skirt and a cream-colored cashmere sweater. A large terra cotta pot containing a flowering plant on a tall stock was cradled in her arms. "Yes, come in, Dee. Let me take care of this orchid."

Dee followed Mrs. Lockwood down the long front hallway. "What an unusual plant," she said, peeking into the living room. "Is that really an orchid?"

"Yes, it is. Just keep following me. The greenhouse is in back."

The hallway led past several other rooms, all filled with antique furniture. "Oh my! I remember some of this furniture," Louisa whispered.

"Sshhh," Dee warned. "This is no time to be admiring the furniture. You're here to do some spying."

The greenhouse was made entirely of large glass squares. A wooden table that stretched the length of the room was almost completely covered by potted plants.

Dee unzipped her vest. The temperature in the greenhouse must have been at least eighty degrees!

"I spend all my time back here," Mrs. Lockwood said. Her smile revealed perfect, white teeth. "I hardly know what's going on in the rest of the house."

"It's a beautiful greenhouse," Dee said.

"Now what was it you wanted to see me about?" Mrs. Lockwood asked.

"Well . . . I uh . . ." Think fast, Dee, she told herself. She had to stall, had to give Louisa time to look around. "Um . . . are these all orchids?"

"Yes. I just love orchids." Mrs. Lockwood rubbed a leaf fondly. "Do you know orchids? This tall one I was carrying is a Cymbidium. The flowers grow on a stalk."

"It's really beautiful," Dee said, taking her

time, slowly admiring the creamy flowers with the dark speckles inside.

"Now, how can I help you?" Mrs. Lockwood asked.

"And what are these called, over here?" Dee asked, moving down the table.

"These are Cattleya." Mrs. Lockwood moved with Dee. "I guess these are what people think of when they picture orchids. Orchids are very hard to grow, you know, especially in this climate."

"They're beautiful," Dee said. She began to wonder how much more there was to say about orchids.

"My son Harry thinks I'm crazy to devote all my time to my orchids," Mrs. Lockwood confided, as she picked up a small trowel and began digging up the dirt around a plant. "But I always tell him, what else should I do? Sit around and watch TV all day? My orchids are so much more beautiful than anything I could see on television."

"They *are* beautiful. Please don't stop. I want to hear more. These orchids are really interesting," Dee said, hoping she sounded sincere.

"Well, bless you," Mrs. Lockwood said, smiling. "I'm so glad you're interested in my orchids. Most people just think I'm a total bore on the subject." And she moved down the table, describing each plant as she went, pointing with her trowel.

Dee stifled a yawn as Mrs. Lockwood's voice droned on. Where was Louisa? What was taking her so long. Dee fought off another yawn. The greenhouse was so hot.

Suddenly, she felt a soft stirring in the moist, warm air. And then she heard Louisa's voice whispering urgently into her ear.

"Dee—the attic!"

"She's back!" Dee thought. And just in time. Mrs. Lockwood had practically run out of orchids to describe!

"There is a whole trunk full of scrapbooks and photo albums in the attic. I *know* they will be helpful," Louisa's voice rose excitedly.

Suddenly Mrs. Lockwood's expression changed and she put down the trowel. Dee's heart began to pound. Had the woman overheard Louisa?

But Mrs. Lockwood was giving Dee an embarrassed smile. "I'm afraid I've been rude," she said, shaking her head. "I forgot to ask about your aunt. How is Winnifred? I usually run into her in town. But since it's gotten colder, my son's been doing my shopping for me."

"Aunt Win is fine," Dee said. "She . . . uh . . . said to say hello."

"Well, I've been so busy talking about my orchids, I haven't given you a moment to tell me the reason for your visit." She wiped her hands on the sides of her tweed skirt, even though they were clean.

Dee smiled, frantically trying to think of an excuse to get up to the attic.

"Yes, dear?"

"Well, it's about a school project," Dee said after an uncomfortably long silence. "I want . . . to write something about the history of Misty Island. Aunt Win told me your family has lived here for a long, long time. I thought maybe I could write the history of the Lockwood family."

"Aren't you the eager beaver," Mrs. Lockwood said encouragingly. "School doesn't even start till the week after next."

"I know. But I hoped to get the research done before I got real busy with homework and stuff," Dee said.

"Well, I don't know how helpful I can be," Mrs. Lockwood said, frowning with concentration. She picked up the trowel and tapped it against the side of a flowerpot. "I'd like to help you out, Dee. But I really don't have time. I was just starting to water my orchids when you arrived. And I have to do some repotting today and—" Suddenly her eyes lit up, and she interrupted herself. "Oh, I know!" She tossed the trowel back onto the table and wiped her hands on her skirt again. "The scrapbooks."

"Scrapbooks?" Dee asked innocently.

"Yes. I used to have all these old scrapbooks and photo albums. But I haven't seen them in ages." Her face fell. "Sorry. I'm afraid I can't help you. I don't know where those scrapbooks are."

"Could you have stored them away somewhere maybe?" Dee prompted her.

Mrs. Lockwood shook her head. Her eyes remained blank. "Maybe. I just can't remember where. It's been such a long time, you see."

"Is there a basement?" Dee asked, trying to lead Mrs. Lockwood to the answer Louisa had already given her. "Could you have stored them in the basement somewhere? Or maybe in the attic. That's where most—"

"The attic!" Mrs. Lockwood cried happily. "Of course! That's exactly where they'd be, you clever girl. I don't know why I didn't think of it myself. Why don't you just go up there now and take a look?"

"Could I? That would be great!" Dee gratefully exclaimed.

"There's a whole lot of old papers up there in a big steamer trunk. You might get lucky and find just what you need," Mrs. Lockwood said, ushering Dee out of the greenhouse and down a narrow back hallway. Dee shivered from the sudden drop in temperature. "If you need me for anything," Mrs. Lockwood offered, "just give a yell. I'll be in the greenhouse."

"Thanks, Mrs. Lockwood," Dee said, starting up the steep, wooden steps to the attic. "This is very nice of you."

Dee stopped at the top of the stairs and looked around. It was pitch black in the narrow hallway. She couldn't see a thing, but once again she felt a soft presence at her side. "Sure smells like an attic," she said to Louisa. She found a light switch on the wall beside her and clicked it on. A dim yellow bulb flickered to life against the opposite wall.

"I know I'll be able to find out who my other relatives are from the photographs and scrapbooks up here," the invisible Louisa said excitedly.

Dee peeked into the attic. She saw that it was one long room, divided by tall screens and stacks of old cartons that reached nearly to the ceiling. Several pieces of furniture were covered with dropcloths. An assortment of old fishing poles, stringless and bent, were propped against an antique dresser. And stacks of yellowing magazines and newspapers littered the floor, along with various sized wooden crates.

Everything was covered with a thick, gray layer of dust. Silvery cobwebs seemed to form curtains in all the corners.

"It's a little creepy up here," Dee said, looking for the trunk.

"You don't suppose it's haunted, do you?" Louisa asked.

Dee laughed. "Was that a joke?"

"Yes," Louisa admitted.

"Pretty good," Dee told her.

"Ohh!" Louisa let out a little cry. "Dee—there, by the window!"

Dee turned quickly and saw a dark figure crouched over something by the narrow window. She squinted, trying to make out his features in the dim light. Was it the ragged-looking man they had seen loitering by the front gate? Had he broken into the house to burglarize the attic?

No. The man turned his head, and she recognized him immediately. It was Harry Lockwood, rummaging through the drawers of an antique rolltop desk.

As Dee tried to back up out of his view, she bumped against a rickety table and sent a stack of books clattering to the floor.

Startled, Harry looked up quickly. His eyes froze on Dee. His face filled with surprise—and then anger.

CHAPTER
13

Harry Lockwood quickly shoved something back into the desk and slammed down the rolltop. "Who are you?" he demanded. "And what are you doing up here?"

"Hi," Dee said, taking a few reluctant steps closer to him. "Sorry—I didn't mean to startle you."

"You didn't," he snapped, his dark eyes burning into hers.

"I'm Dee Forest. Your mother—I was just talking to her . . . and . . ."

"And what?" He locked the rolltop with a big, old-fashioned silver key. Then he shoved the key into his trouser pocket and turned back to Dee.

"And she said there were some scrapbooks and photo albums I could look at up here."

He brushed a hand back through his slicked-down hair. "Scrapbooks? We don't have any scrapbooks. My mother must be mistaken."

"She said they were in a steamer trunk."

"Well, maybe," he said, scowling. "What do you want these scrapbooks for?" he asked seriously.

"I want to write a report about the history of the Lockwoods on Misty Island."

"That should be a real boring report," he sneered. Then he headed toward the stairs. "Well, go ahead. Good luck finding anything in this mess." He stopped on the third step down and turned back. "Who are you, anyway? You're not from around here, are you?"

"No. I'm from Cambridge. I'm staying with my aunt—Winnifred Forest—for the winter," Dee told him.

"Well, okay," he said. "Be careful with those scrapbooks if you find them. They're valuable. And don't steal anything!" He clomped heavily down the stairs.

"Nice guy," Dee muttered as soon as he was gone.

"What was he doing over at that desk?" Louisa wondered aloud as she slowly materialized. Her old-fashioned blouse and jumper looked just right to Dee for a change, among all the old furniture. "He acted very guilty of something when he first saw you. Wouldn't you say so?"

"He sure did," Dee agreed. "Something strange is going on here, Louisa. First the ragged man outside the gate, then Harry up here in the attic." She walked over to the desk and tried pushing back the rolltop, but it wouldn't budge.

"He locked it," Louisa said. "Perhaps he was hiding something in here."

"Or stealing something from it," Dee suggested. "Maybe that's how Harry can afford his fancy fur coat and sportscar. Maybe he steals things from his own mother's house."

"No. That cannot be!" Louisa looked truly shocked. "But that Dodge boy in the fish store did hint that there was something . . . "

"If only we could catch Harry in the act," Dee said, already believing her theory about him. "If we actually caught him stealing, that would really be a help to Mrs. Lockwood," Dee said, pacing the floor. The ancient pine planks creaked beneath her sneakers. "And that would mean you had helped one relative. It would be your first step to rejoining your family, Louisa."

Louisa sighed and sat down on a trunk. "I really appreciate your sympathy and encouragement, Dee," she said. "Those are wonderful qualities for a friend to have. But I'm afraid it's hopeless. I don't even know how to begin."

"You can begin by standing up," Dee told her.

"What?"

"Stand up."

"All right." Louisa stood up. "Why?"

"Because you were sitting on the trunk!"

Sure enough, Louisa had been perched on a black steamer trunk. Each girl tugged on a latch, trying to get it open. The latches came up without much trouble, but the heavy lid seemed to be stuck. No matter how hard the girls tried, they couldn't budge it.

"We need something to pry this open," Dee said.

"It opened easily enough when I was here before," Louisa said.

"Well, it's closed now," Dee muttered.

"I have an idea," Louisa said, suddenly looking pleased with herself. "I've never tried anything like this, but it might accomplish the task. I'm going to try pushing it open from the inside."

"Huh?" Dee wasn't sure she'd heard right. But Louisa was already disappearing—through the solid side of the trunk!

A few seconds later, Dee heard her muffled voice coming from inside. The sound was more ghostly than usual. "You pull, and I'll push," Louisa called.

Dee pulled with all her might and almost fell over when the lid popped right open. She quickly regained her balance, automatically wrinkling her nose against the musty smell of decaying paper. "Louisa, you clever ghost! You did it!"

A few seconds later, Louisa reappeared at Dee's side. The two girls stared hopefully down into the trunk. It was filled nearly to the top with yellowing documents: old bills; newspapers; magazines; theater playbills from the 1930's; a crumbling telephone directory; and stacks of old letters wrapped in faded pink ribbons. At the bottom of all this, were several large scrapbooks and dog-eared photo albums.

"We've found them!" Dee cried.

"Don't get your hopes up, Dee," Louisa warned. "I didn't really look through these before. There might not be anything useful in them. What exactly are we looking for, anyway?"

"Information," Dee said, eagerly snatching the photo album and setting it down on the floor between them. "Any information that will help you help your relatives."

She turned the album so that they were starting in the back with the most recent photographs. "Look! There's Mrs. Lockwood."

The photos on the last page were labeled "September, 1965." They had obviously been taken in front of the Lockwood house by the white picket fence. The house looked exactly the same then as it did now, and Mrs. Lockwood looked only slightly younger in the photos. She had the same wavy brown hair in the same style; but instead of her conservative brown tweeds, she was wearing blue denim bell-bottom jeans and a colorfully embroidered peasant blouse. There were two little boys standing next to her.

"The one on the left has to be Harry," Dee exclaimed. "See—he had a nasty look about him even then! I bet he was a real little brat."

Louisa stared intently at the photographs.

"They're so remarkably clear," she said. "And they're in color, almost as real as life."

"Who do you think the other little boy could be?" Dee asked thoughtfully. "Do you suppose Harry has a brother?"

Louisa didn't seem to be listening. Dee saw her reach down for another photo album. With its faded cover and ragged black pages, it looked much older than the one she was holding.

Louisa flipped silently to the front pages of the old album. The photographs there were not very clear, nor were they in color. They had browned over the years until they were shadowy and dark, as if they'd been taken at night.

Louisa stared at the faces in these, the oldest photos. "Oh, my soul!" she cried, her voice filled with emotion.

Dee struggled to see the faces of the people in the faded photographs. They were all dressed in black, which made the photos ever darker. But despite the somber clothes, they all wore bright, beaming smiles on their faces.

The photos were all full-length portraits, taken out of doors. Dee could just barely make out dark shutters against the white wood of a small, square house in the photo's background.

"That's my family," Louisa finally managed

to say, her eyes darting from one photograph to the next. "That's my father." The man in the picture had a bushy mustache and was wearing a fisherman's cap. "And that's my mother—and Edward, my brother!"

"Is that your house in the background?" Dee asked, staring hard at the old photos, trying to absorb every detail.

"Yes," Louisa said. "I'll never forget this day. It was so exciting. Everyone knew that a photographer was coming from Boston. We all dressed up in our best finery. The day was beautiful and sunny. We all wanted to see what it was like to have a photograph taken. Everyone on the island came to watch, came to be photographed.

"I can still hear the photographer yelling to us, 'Be still! Be perfectly still!' We had to stand that way for so long, several minutes at least, without moving a muscle."

"Wow! This is amazing!" Dee cried. "And look, Louisa, there you are!"

Dee felt goosebumps all over as she stared at the photo of Louisa. It had been taken nearly a hundred years before, but Louisa looked exactly the same. Her hair was the same. Her face was the same. Even her clothes were the same—the white puff-sleeved blouse, the long black jumper. The picture must have been taken shortly before her death.

Dee shivered. Her heart suddenly began to pound. "I'm in this attic with a ghost," she told herself, feeling a stab of icy fear, the kind of fear she had felt when she first encountered Louisa. She stared at the picture of the dead girl. *Dead, dead, dead.*

Suddenly she felt something warm and wet dripping onto her arm. She looked up in surprise. A wave of sadness swept over Dee, and her fear instantly melted away as she realized Louisa was crying.

Louisa Lockwood might be a ghost. But her tears were real and very human.

CHAPTER
14

"This spying business isn't as exciting as I thought it would be," Dee said disgustedly.

"Oh, I don't know," Louisa said. "I think it's fun. I like being out at night."

"Shh!" Dee whispered, even though no one was around.

The two girls were crouching behind a tall, untrimmed hedge across the road from the Lockwood house on a cold, moonless Saturday night. This was their third night of watching and waiting.

Dee glanced at her watch. The time was nearly eleven o'clock. Three nights in a row they had waited for Aunt Win to go to bed.

Then they had snuck out in the darkness to spy on Harry and catch him doing whatever malicious, evil thing he *had* to be doing.

But for three nights in a row, Harry had failed to appear.

The wind picked up, causing the trees to shiver and whisper. Dee pulled her blue and white striped hat down over her ears. "It sure is dark," she said.

"I like the dark," Louisa declared, allowing herself to float up above the hedge. "I'm a ghost, aren't I?" She floated higher until she was nearly as high as the attic window across the street.

"Louisa—come down!" Dee called nervously. "Someone might see you!"

"You're just jealous," Louisa teased. But she floated back down behind the hedge.

"You're very giddy tonight, Louisa."

"Spying is fun," Louisa said. "I never snuck out of the house or did anything like this when I was alive."

"Well, maybe it isn't such a good idea," Dee said, changing her position. "Both my legs are asleep, and it's cold out here. And we've spent three nights spying on nothing."

"I know what you'd rather be doing," Louisa

teased. "You'd rather be going for a walk with Nicky Dodge!"

"Louisa!" Dee made a face. "I only went for a walk with him yesterday afternoon because I had no choice. He showed up at the inn, and I wasn't doing anything at all, so—"

"I think he likes you," Louisa interrupted, floating up off the ground again. "When he asked you to go for a walk with him, he was as red as one of his father's lobsters!"

Dee started to laugh. Nicky *had* looked like a big lobster. Louisa, floating casually over the hedge, began to giggle, too.

They were still giggling when two headlights came around the curve of the road, and they saw the green Jaguar pull up to the gate across the street.

"It's him!" Dee hissed, grabbing Louisa's hand to pull her down behind the hedge.

Louisa immediately vanished!

Still holding on to the invisible hand, Dee watched Harry climb out of the car, open the gate, and get back behind the wheel. Before pulling up the drive, he turned off the car's headlights. Then he drove slowly, very slowly, up to the house.

"Come on, let's go!" Louisa whispered, tugging Dee's arm.

"No. He might see us." Dee suddenly felt very afraid. This wasn't a game anymore.

"He definitely won't see me!" Louisa declared.

"Why did he turn off his lights?" Dee wondered aloud as, still holding onto Louisa's hand, she followed her across the road and slipped through the open gate.

"Perhaps he doesn't want his mother to know he's home," Louisa replied.

"I'll bet you're right," Dee said.

Standing just inside the gate, they watched Harry stop the Jaguar near the front walk. A few seconds later, he climbed out of the car, closing the door silently. Then, instead of taking the flagstone walk to the front door, he jogged quickly toward the back of the house.

"Let's follow him," Louisa whispered. "Isn't it a shame you can't be invisible, too."

"It sure is!" Dee agreed. Cold and frightened, she suddenly wanted to turn around and run away. But she knew she couldn't desert Louisa. She had to help her.

Dee ran quietly over the wet, fallen leaves, her sneakers squishing in the soft ground. She watched from the shadows as Harry darted through a side door near the back of the house. Seconds later, a light went on.

Dee ran up to the door. Breathing hard, more from the excitement than the exertion, she hesitated for a moment. "Stick close," she told Louisa. Then she opened the door and slipped inside.

Dee found herself in a narrow back hallway filled with mops, brooms, and shelves of cleaning supplies. Beyond the hallway, she could see the large kitchen. To her right, a stairway led up to the second floor. She could hear the stairs creaking and shifting under Harry Lockwood's shoes.

"Upstairs, Louisa," she whispered, already starting to climb.

Was this crazy? Dee wondered. Yes. Of course, it was. But Harry was sneaking into his own house. That meant he had to be up to no good.

Dee took a deep breath and, trying to be as silent as possible on the squeaky, old stairway, followed the sound of Harry's footsteps up to the attic.

Despite the chill of the night, the attic was uncomfortably overheated, the air heavy with dust and decay. Dee uttered a soft gasp. Did something move under that blanket in the corner? She inhaled deeply and almost forgot to breathe again.

Dee forced herself to move forward. She took a few silent steps and bumped into something, banging her knee painfully.

Startled, she nearly cried out again. But, looking down, she saw that it was only a child's rocking chair and kept going.

A low-watt lamp cast yellow light against the far wall. Tall, black shadows climbed to the ceiling like bent and twisted trees, making the room seem more like a jungle than an attic.

Dee inched her way carefully toward the light to avoid bumping into anything else. A floorboard groaned beneath her sneakers. She stopped and held her breath again.

Had Harry heard that? No. He hadn't called out. After a few minutes of stillness, Dee took a few more steps, and then Harry came into view.

He was bent over the rolltop desk again, fiddling with the lock. The yellow light made his dark eyes gleam with intensity. His face was expressionless, but his trembling hands revealed his eagerness.

Ducking behind a stack of cartons, Dee watched him turn the old-fashioned metal key and roll up the desk top. He reached inside the desk and withdrew a black velvet pouch, and Dee noticed that his hands were gloved.

"He *must* be stealing," she said to herself. "Why else is he keeping his gloves on in the house?"

"We've got to stop him," Dee whispered to Louisa.

"We can't," Louisa whispered from behind.

But Dee wasn't so sure. "Maybe *we* can't," she agreed. "But *you* can. You're a ghost, Louisa!" Dee hissed. "*Haunt* him!"

CHAPTER

15

Dee caught her breath as a stained old sheet that had been covering an antique armchair rose up in the air and floated toward Harry. As it came closer, it began to take human shape—a head bobbed in its center, and arms raised at both sides.

"Oh no!" Dee groaned to herself. "Not the corny old sheet routine! He'll never fall for that!"

She shook her head in dismay as the sheet, its ends dragging limply across the floor, drifted silently up to Harry. The sight was about as scary as a kindergarten kid's Halloween costume.

At first, Harry didn't even notice his ghostly

visitor. He'd opened the velvet pouch and was holding it up to the yellow light, totally absorbed in examining its contents.

When he finally did look up, he cried out in surprise and the bag clanked heavily back onto the desk's top. Gold coins spilled out onto the desk. "Hey!" he yelled, sounding more angry than frightened. Eyes on the approaching apparition, he hurriedly scooped the coins back into the pouch.

He took a step back as the ghost floated closer, his mouth turning down in disbelief, his eyes staring straight ahead at the visitor. Then, without warning, Harry pounced. Both hands shot out at once, and he jerked the sheet, as if pulling a tablecloth off a dinner table.

"Let's take a look at you!" he growled. "Let's see what—"

Harry broke off in surprise. There was no one to see! He examined the sheet, then rolled it into a ball and angrily tossed it at the wall. Shaking his head as if to dismiss the whole thing, he picked up the pouch again.

"It didn't work," Louisa whispered, back at Dee's side once more. "Now what?"

"How about some floating furniture?" Dee urged. Harry was already pulling the string on the pouch, closing it tight. "Hurry! Do something. Start howling, Louisa!"

"No—please—I've never howled in my life. I don't think I can!" Louisa whispered.

"Okay. You take care of the furniture. *I'll* do the howling," Dee whispered back.

Meanwhile, Harry was already walking toward the back stairs, the pouch tucked snugly under his arm. He spun around, startled, when Louisa suddenly slammed the rolltop desk shut. Then he stopped, frozen with disbelief, as a ratty, fox fur cape lifted itself out of a carton and began swaying in the air.

"Owooooooooo!" Dee began to howl.

The fur cape dropped to the floor at Harry's feet, just as a headless dressmaker's dummy came to life, scooting across the floor.

"Owooooooooo!" Dee's howl was loud enough to rattle the windows!

Two fishing nets drifted up from where they had been resting against the wall and began sailing in Harry's direction.

"No! Get away from me!" he cried, his face finally filled with fear.

The nets floated closer. Dee's howls grew shriller.

Panic-stricken, Harry dropped the pouch, turned, and scrambled down the stairs.

The nets drifted down to the floor, lifeless again. The howling ceased. The only sound was that of Harry's shoes clambering down the back stairs.

Dee and Louisa remained silent until they could no longer hear his footsteps. Then they both burst out laughing, celebrating their triumph and Louisa's first attempt at haunting someone.

"Did you see the look on his face?" Dee cried. "I thought his eyes were going to pop!"

"He was terribly frightened," Louisa agreed. "I thought your ghostly sounds were most convincing."

"Thank you," Dee said, still laughing. "We make a great ghost team." She suddenly remembered the velvet pouch. "Come on. Let's see what he was stealing."

She dashed over to the pouch, which Harry had dropped at the head of the stairs. Bending over in the darkness, she reached to pick it up—

And another pair of hands reached for it at the same time!

"You!" Harry cried, his face white with fury.

He had apparently run back up the stairs and was now leaning over the top step, breathing heavily, but clearly in control again.

Dee let out a little cry and started to back away. But he grabbed her arms and dragged her toward the stairs.

"I never did believe in ghosts," he snarled, jerking her hard and throwing her off balance.

Dee fell to her knees. Harry scooped up his pouch and then pulled Dee onto the stairway. Clamping a hand over her mouth, he held her prisoner against his side. Her face pressed against the big fur coat, Dee was nearly overwhelmed by the smell of stale tobacco. But it wasn't the smell that made her flinch—it was fear.

Now Dee really felt like howling!

CHAPTER
16

Keeping a gloved hand tight over her mouth, Harry dragged Dee out the side door and to his car. She struggled hard at first but gave up when she realized that he was much too strong for her. There was no way she could break his grip.

Harry shoved Dee into the driver's seat and squeezed in after her. "Where are you taking me?" she cried. Before he could answer, she grabbed for the door handle on the other side and pushed hard. But the door was already locked.

"Somewhere safe," he replied calmly, starting the car. "What are you so scared of? You're a ghost, aren't you?"

Dee thought of Louisa. Was she in the car with them? Was she still up in the attic, too frightened to follow? Dee sat there, silently listening for a sign of Louisa's presence, as Harry backed down the driveway and through the open gate.

The next twenty minutes were the most terrifying of Dee's life. Harry drove at breakneck speed down the middle of the narrow, curving road that circled Misty Island. The tires squealed as he spun around the curves, never veering from the yellow center line. The road's surface was slick with dew, and Harry had to move the wheel constantly to keep the car from skidding.

Dee closed her eyes, waiting for the inevitable collision with an oncoming car, waiting for Harry to lose control, for the squeal of brakes, the crash . . . waiting for the end.

But there were no other cars on the road. Few people went out near midnight on Misty Island—there was no place to go. Dee felt as if she were inside a bullet that was being shot across the island, past the dark willows bending in the wind, past the pine-covered woods and the jutting rocks—shot away from everyone she knew, far away from her safe, warm world.

Suddenly the car phone rang shrilly. Startled, Dee opened her eyes to see Harry grabbing the phone with his right hand, while his left worked hard to keep the speeding car on the road.

"Yeah. Yeah, it's me," Harry snarled. "Yeah. I got them. Why are you such a worrier? I told you I'd get the coins. The whole collection."

There was a long silence, and then Harry shouted, "What?" into the phone. He was obviously having trouble hearing over the wind roaring past the car. "I'm telling you, don't worry. I've had a slight delay—" he glared at Dee—"but no problem. I'll be out of here first thing in the morning. That's right. The early ferry. If you want the gold, you'd better be there when I get off, hear? And you'd better have the cash with you. Now stop worrying." He slammed down the phone.

Moments later the car screeched to a stop, sliding for what seemed like miles over wet sand. "Get out!" Harry ordered.

"Where are we?" Dee asked. She stared out of the car window but saw only darkness.

"Get out," he repeated, reaching across Dee and pushing open her door. She heard the sound of waves breaking on the shore and realized he had taken her to the beach on the other side of the island. But why? Was he going to drown her?

"Welcome to Fingers Cove," Harry said. He climbed quickly out of the car, hurried around to the passenger side, and pulled Dee roughly from her seat. "Don't bother screaming for help. No one comes to this deserted place at night."

"Let me go," Dee insisted, trying to sound a lot braver than she was feeling.

He laughed, his nostrils flaring. The wind, wet and heavy with salt, swirled around them.

"What are you going to do? Are you going to—kill me?" He spat on the sand, just missing her sneaker. "No need," he gloated, tightening his grip. "I just have to keep you out of the way for a few hours."

Dee tried to dig her heels into the sand as he started dragging her along the beach, but Harry hardly seemed to notice. "Now where is that place?" he muttered to himself. "There's a deserted, old shack somewhere by the trees," he said, searching the dark treeline. "We used to play there when we were kids. . . . Hey, there it is!"

"Listen, I promise I won't say a word," Dee

said, desperate to get away from this cold beach, desperate not to be locked in some horrible, deserted shack.

"Go ahead. Say a word," he snickered. "Say all the words you want. No one can hear you out here. There's no one living within ten miles of this cove."

This isn't happening to me, Dee thought, as she was dragged over the wet sand. *This can't be happening. Aunt Win—somebody—please wake me out of this awful nightmare. Louisa—where are you?*

The shack appeared to be built of boards that had washed ashore. The doorway was so low, Dee had to bend her head to enter. Inside, it smelled of fish and rotting wood.

Harry shined a penlight around the tiny room. The walls were hung with fish nets. A tiny, kerosene stove stood in one corner. Old newspapers and books were piled on a wooden crate beside it. A paper plate piled high with fishbones sat on another crate.

"Someone's been here," Harry observed. "Kids, probably."

"I don't want to stay here," Dee said flatly, her fear turning to anger.

"That's too bad, isn't it?" he growled. Then

a smile flickered across his face. "Hey, I've got one question. How'd you do that in the attic?"

"Do what?"

"You really had me going for a minute. How'd you make those things float around like that?"

"Oh. That," Dee said. "It was easy. I had an invisible friend with me."

Where *was* Louisa? Dee wondered again.

"Ho ho. Very funny," Harry said sarcastically. With a surprisingly quick move, he pulled down a fish net and began wrapping it around her. "I don't have a rope. This'll have to do."

"No!" Dee screamed desperately as he circled her with the foul-smelling net.

Dee struggled wildly, but he pulled it tighter and tighter around her body, wrapping her arms inside it. She would soon be as immobile as a mummy.

"No!" She twisted around with all her strength, trying to break free from the net. "You'll never get away with this! I'll tell the police."

He laughed. "By the time they find you—*if* they ever find you—I'll be hundreds of miles away from here. And I'll be rich."

Dee managed to break free for a moment,

but immediately tripped over the net. She started to fall, couldn't move her hands to catch herself, and dropped like a stone to the floor.

Dee's head hit the side of a crate. And then everything went black.

CHAPTER
17

"Dee. . . . Wake up!"

Louisa gently lifted Dee's head. "Wake up, Dee. Can you hear me?"

Dee groaned and opened her eyes.

"Oh, Dee. Thank goodness you're alive. I was so worried."

Dee groaned again and tried to sit up, but her head felt like a two-ton weight. She sank back onto the floor and closed her eyes.

"I was so frightened," Louisa said, cradling her friend's head. "The horseless carriage—it went so fast. It made me very dizzy. I kept thinking that at any moment we would sail off the road and fly up into the trees!"

Dee groaned in response. Louisa's voice

sounded so far away. She concentrated on bringing it closer.

"I was so frightened," Louisa repeated. "I wanted to help, but I didn't know what to do. We were going so fast. I—I closed my eyes. I couldn't move. Can you hear me, Dee? Are you all right?"

Dee hunched her shoulders and groaned again. She wanted to sit up. Why wouldn't her body cooperate?

A scraping sound outside made Louisa jump to her feet. Dee opened her eyes. "Louisa, what is it? Is Harry still here?"

"Sshhhh." Louisa put her finger to her lips. "There's someone outside the door," she whispered. She listened some more. The sound repeated. "Maybe it's just an animal," Louisa said hopefully. "Or the wind."

"What?" Dee tried to sit up, but the whole room was spinning. The back of her head throbbed painfully.

"Oh no!" Louisa cried, her voice filled with terror. "Get up, Dee! Please, get up!"

And then Louisa vanished just as a tall figure lumbered into the shack.

CHAPTER
18

Dee forced herself up on one elbow, but the fish net that bound her was too tight and the pain in her head was too intense. With a groan, she lay back down again. "Who's there?" She tried to yell, but her voice came out weak and small. She wasn't even sure the man had heard her.

He hadn't seen her yet, either. Without hesitation, he stepped into the shack and walked over to one of the upturned crates that served as a table.

Squinting against the pain, Dee watched him reach for a lantern on the crate and then strike a wooden match. Almost instantly, a flickering orange light pierced the darkness of the tiny room.

Smoke from the lantern filtered up over the man's face, half of which was hidden in shadow. But Dee recognized him at once. It wasn't Harry—it was the ragged man she and Louisa had seen in front of Mrs. Lockwood's gate.

Would he remember her? Dee wondered. Would he remember that she had chased him away? Would he take his revenge on her now?

She gritted her teeth and pulled herself into a sitting position, struggling against the tightly wrapped fish net. "Hey!" he cried out, finally noticing her down on the floor.

He picked up the lantern and slowly moved toward Dee, his stubbled face expressionless. She tried to back away from him, but the net held her prisoner. There was nowhere she could go. *Now* where was Louisa? "Help me," Dee cried. Again the words came out faint, barely audible. She stared up into the man's dark eyes, trying to read his thoughts, trying to decide if he meant to do her harm.

The man set the lantern on the floor and bent down beside Dee. Behind him, Dee was relieved to see the coffee pot lift up off the small kerosene stove and hover over the man's head. Louisa obviously planned to bean him with it if he made a wrong move.

Dee groaned as the room started to spin again.

The man frowned, but he didn't say a word.

He's going to kill me, Dee thought. She stared up at him, waiting, praying for Louisa to bring the coffee pot down on his head.

Then, without warning, the man reached out his large, slender hand and very carefully began to examine Dee's forehead. "You've got a pretty bad cut there," he said, frowning harder as he stared at her left temple.

He climbed slowly to his feet, his head narrowly missing the coffee pot that secretly hovered over him.

Dee breathed a sigh of relief. He didn't seem to want to hurt her. But what was he going to do?

She watched him pull something out of a crate and dunk it in a nearby bucket. When he turned around, Dee saw that he was holding a wet cloth. He bent back down over her and began cleaning the cut on her temple.

"Harry did a really good job on you," he said, his deep voice revealing no emotion.

"What?" Dee cried, startled. Did he know Harry Lockwood? Had he been here all along? Was he working with Harry? Maybe he *did* want to hurt her.

Dee's eyes opened wide as the coffee pot suddenly floated back onto the stove. Louisa must have decided that this wild-haired, ragged man was no threat. But Dee wasn't so sure.

She turned her head to the side as the man continued to dab at it with the cloth in silence. "Lie still," he said finally, in a harsh tone that confirmed all of Dee's fears.

He's working with Harry Lockwood, she thought. It's his job to keep me here until Harry is safely on the morning ferry. He isn't going to let me out of here. If I try to escape, he'll—

In one quick motion the man stood up and tossed the cloth into the bucket. "Lie still," he repeated. "I'll be coming right back." Then, to Dee's surprise, he turned and lumbered out of the shack.

"Louisa . . . ?" Dee whispered.

"Yes, Dee." Louisa's voice was right beside her.

"See if that man is standing guard outside the shack."

While she waited for Louisa's report, Dee

tried to sit up. Her head still throbbed, but the pain was growing dull, and she no longer felt so dizzy.

"He's running away, down the beach," Louisa's disembodied voice announced. "He seems to be in a really big hurry."

"Good," Dee said. "So are we. We've got to get away from here—fast!"

"Are you feeling better?" Louisa asked as she slowly came into view, a worried expression on her face.

"Yes. Much," Dee said. "I'll be fine as soon as I'm out of this awful net."

Louisa helped Dee to her feet. Then, floating a foot off the ground, she circled her, pulling away the net until Dee was entirely unwrapped.

Dee's legs felt shaky at first, but after taking a few steps, she started to feel a lot steadier. "Okay. Let's go," she said. She peered out the door to the shack. The sky was just starting to lighten.

"It's almost morning," Dee said. "I don't believe it!"

"You were unconscious for quite a while," Louisa told her.

"We'd better get back to the inn. I don't want my aunt to be worried." Dee struggled to think clearly, to figure out the best thing to do. "Maybe we can still stop Harry Lockwood. Maybe Aunt Win can help."

Dee reached for the lantern. "Might as well take this along. It's not quite light out there, yet." Then, still a little unsteady, she bumped into the crate. She caught the lantern before it toppled over, but a book fell off the crate and hit the floor with a thud.

Dee kept moving, but Louisa stopped to look at the book. "It's a Bible!" Louisa exclaimed, surprised. "It looks very old." As she picked up the Bible, several photographs and a folded-up piece of paper slipped out of it. "Wait, Dee," she called. "Look how old this is. It looks just like the one my family had when I was a little girl."

"Come on, Louisa!" Dee cried. "Let's get out of here."

But Louisa was busy unfolding the sheet of paper. "It's a family tree," she said, scanning the names on the old document. "Oh my soul! It's *my* family tree! The Lockwood family."

"How strange," Dee said, taking a few steps closer and lowering the lantern so they could see the photographs better.

One of the photos was in color. It showed

Mrs. Lockwood standing in front of her house, flanked by two teenage boys. Harry stood on one side, dressed in jeans and a turtleneck sweater. He looked younger, but not much different. The photo was eight or nine years old, at most.

On Mrs. Lockwood's other side stood a smiling older boy who bore a striking resemblance to Harry. Both Dee and Louisa recognized him at the same time. The boy in the photo was clearly the ragged man who lived in this shack!

"He must be Harry Lockwood's brother!" Dee exclaimed, as she slipped the photograph back into the old Bible. "That means he's definitely working with Harry. Come on, Louisa, we've got to get away—now!"

CHAPTER
19

Still carrying the lantern, Dee ran out onto the beach, and Louisa followed. Tall waves crashed against the shore, sending up a white spray that was carried along on the wind. The sun was a little higher now, slowly burning through the gray morning haze.

"We won't need this," Dee said, dropping the lantern and heading for the road.

They scrambled over the low dunes, the wind at their backs. Dee walked and then jogged, her sneakers crunching over the wet sand.

When they got to the road, they stopped for a moment so Dee could catch her breath and figure out which way to go. They were on the opposite end of Misty Island from her aunt's inn, she knew. The road led in a circle—but which way was shorter?

She had just decided to follow the road to the left when she saw a pair of dim yellow headlights cutting through the haze. "Someone's coming!"

"Hide, Dee! Maybe it's Harry Lockwood," Louisa said, vanishing once more.

The headlights got larger and brighter as the car sped toward them. Dee looked for a place to hide. But the ground was flat here and the high grass along the road was too sparse to conceal her.

Dee stood there like a deer trapped in the headlights, heart pounding, as the car came into view. But it wasn't Harry's Jaguar. It was a blue and white police car!

Dee waved frantically and called out to it, but the car was already past her. Then it squealed to a stop, sliding over the sandy road.

The driver's door swung open, and Officer Munroe, the town constable, pulled his bulky frame out. "Do you need help, miss?"

"Yes!" Dee cried, and began running toward him.

"What are you doing way out here so early? Are you lost?" Munroe looked suspicious.

"No. I mean, yes," Dee told him. She didn't know where to begin. "I was brought here. I mean, I was kidnapped. I—"

"Slow down, please." He put a hand on her shoulder. "And get in the car. It's cold out here." He walked around to the passenger side and opened the door. Dee slid gratefully into the front seat. Munroe walked around and eased himself back down behind the wheel.

He had a cup of coffee on the dashboard. "Here," he said, handing it to her.

Dee took a sip, made a face, and handed it back to him. She wondered if Louisa was in the car and decided she must be.

"We've got to hurry," Dee said. "Harry Lockwood is taking the morning ferry. We've got to stop him."

"Whoa. Hold your horses," Munroe said, taking a long sip of coffee. "Aren't you Winnifred Forest's niece, the one visiting from Boston?"

"Yes," Dee said impatiently. "But we've got to hurry. Harry will get away. He's got the gold coins."

Munroe carefully replaced the cup on the dashboard. Then he gave Dee a long, serious look.

"I know it sounds crazy," Dee told him. "But we've got to get to the dock right away. Really!"

"Have you been out all night?" Munroe asked, ignoring her impatience.

"Yes, but that's not important," Dee insisted. "I'm trying to tell you—"

"You can tell me the whole story while I drive you to your aunt's," Munroe broke in, throwing the car into reverse and turning it around on the narrow road. "She'll be frantic if she wakes up and sees you're not there. Why don't we just let her know you're okay. Then we can go to the dock, if you still want to."

He stamped on the gas pedal and the patrol car lurched forward with a jolt. The dunes rolled quickly by and were replaced by a blur of pine trees.

Munroe drove silently, his eyes straight ahead, expertly maneuvering over the curving road. Dee wanted to tell him exactly what had happened, but she couldn't decide where to start.

She couldn't admit she'd been spying on Harry Lockwood for three days, couldn't reveal how she knew about the gold coins, couldn't even mention Louisa. . . . So most of her story was missing right from the beginning.

Dee did her best to make sense, talking as slowly and calmly as she could. Munroe nodded his head from time to time, but after a while, Dee got the idea that he wasn't even listening. "You've just got to trust me," she finally said in frustration. "We've got to get to the dock in time to stop Harry from escaping with his mother's coins."

Munroe didn't reply. He simply stopped the car. Dee was amazed to find herself back at the inn.

Munroe took another sip of his coffee, then lifted himself out of the car. Dee barely had her door open before her aunt was running down the driveway.

"Dee—what on earth!" Win called. "When you weren't in your room, I didn't know what to think! Are you okay?"

Then she hugged Dee so tightly, Dee couldn't answer.

"Where in the world have you been?" Aunt Winnifred demanded, slowly releasing her niece. "Your father would *kill* me if he found out that I—that you—that we . . ."

"I'm fine," Dee assured her. "Really."

"I found her out by the cove," Officer Munroe reported.

"But why didn't you tell me you were going out?" Aunt Win asked Dee. "Why did you go out in the middle of the night? And what happened to your head?"

Dee lifted a shaky hand to her head. "I'm fine. Really," Dee said. "I'll tell you all about it later. Right now is not the time. But there may still be time to stop Harry."

"Harry?" Aunt Win reached up and fluffed out her orange hair with both hands. "Harry Lockwood? What has *he* got to do with this?"

"She keeps saying something about stopping Harry at the ferry dock," Munroe said quietly.

"Please, let's just get to the dock," Dee insisted. "We've got to stop him!"

"She received a bad bump on the head," Munroe told Win, talking about Dee as if she weren't there. "Maybe it affected her mind a little. You know. A concussion or something."

Aunt Win shook her head. "Oh no. If Dee says we have to stop Harry Lockwood at the pier, I believe her," she told the police officer firmly. "There's nothing the matter with my niece's mind!"

Munroe took a step back. He knew he'd been

challenged, and it was obvious he didn't want to tangle with Winnifred Forest.

"Let's get going," Win said, putting her arm around Dee's shoulders and starting toward the police car.

"Well, I really don't think you need to come along," Munroe said. "I'm sure I can handle this myself."

"Nothing doing, Munroe. I'm not missing out on the excitement," Aunt Win said, and then she added, "whatever it turns out to be."

"Well, I'm not driving you, Win." She had pushed Munroe too far. He decided to be obstinate. "Because then I'll just have to take you home again when it turns out there's no one on the dock."

"Fine, Munroe." Aunt Win spun around and headed up the driveway, pulling Dee with her. "I wouldn't want you wasting the taxpayers' money on unnecessary gas!" she added sarcastically. "I'll take my jeep, and we'll meet you there."

Munroe rolled his eyes and sighed wearily. Then he lowered himself into the patrol car, started it up, and drove off toward the pier.

Aunt Win practically leaped into the jeep. Dee wondered where she got her energy. "Here we go," Winnifred said, struggling to get the engine started.

"Are you here?" Dee asked, suddenly remembering Louisa.

"Yes," Louisa whispered from the back seat, her voice filled with apprehension at the thought of another terrifying car ride.

"Of course, I'm here," Aunt Win said, a very worried look on her face as she turned to Dee. "Are you *sure* you're okay? Maybe that bump on your head is worse than I thought. Why don't you lie down in the back seat?"

"There's no room," Dee said, and immediately realized she must be *very* tired. She never would have said that if she'd been totally alert.

"No room? You'd have the whole empty seat," Aunt Win protested.

"I meant there's no time," Dee said. "Please hurry. We can't let Harry get away. We can't!"

Aunt Win obediently hurried. Pulling down the long drive, she floored the gas pedal. The jeep lurched forward onto the road and nearly collided with an egg truck coming full speed around the curve.

Aunt Win swerved back onto the sand, the loud honking of the truck horn announcing the driver's displeasure. As soon as the truck was safely past, its horn still wailing, Aunt Win spun the wheel, and they bumped back onto the road.

Driving full speed down the curving, narrow road with the wind roaring through the topless jeep was as exciting as a carnival thrill ride to Dee. And Aunt Win seemed to be having a wonderful time, too. But as Dee ducked down and closed her eyes against the ferocious roar of wind, she wondered how Louisa was doing.

"Look out!" Aunt Win kept shouting over the rushing wind. "Look out!" as a hay wagon started slowly across the road. "Look out!" as two teenagers on horseback shied their horses back to the shoulder. "Look out! Look out!"

Somehow, miraculously, Aunt Win finally slammed on the brakes, and the jeep squealed to a safe stop across from the long wooden dock that served as the island's sole pier.

Dee's face stung from the cold wind. She reached up with one hand and tried to warm her numb, frozen nose.

Munroe's patrol car pulled up behind the jeep. Aunt Win had beaten him to the dock!

Aunt Win opened her door and jumped down to the ground. "Good heavens. Dee was right," she called to Munroe, who was slowly climbing out of his car.

"What?" Dee had trouble getting her cold lips to move.

Aunt Win turned to Dee with a look of surprise. "There goes Harry Lockwood. How did you know he'd be here?"

Standing up in the front seat of the jeep, Dee saw Harry Lockwood running down the dock toward the waiting ferry. He had a large suitcase in one hand.

"Stop him!" Dee cried, jumping out of the jeep. "Somebody stop him!"

At the sound of her voice, Harry stopped short and turned around. His mouth dropped open in surprise when he saw Dee, but he quickly forced a smile onto his face. He waved casually and continued—walking this time— toward the ferry.

"Lockwood! Would you mind coming over here a minute?" Munroe yelled.

"I'm going to be late!" Harry yelled back, just a few yards from his destination. "The ferry's about to leave."

"Spalding will wait for you," Munroe said. "Come over here. It'll only take a minute of your time."

Harry pasted a wide smile on his face and came walking back. "What is it, Munroe? What do you want?" He nodded at Dee and Aunt Win, still smiling.

"This girl has made some serious accusations against you," Munroe said, staring intently into Harry's eyes.

Harry gave Munroe a bewildered look, then turned to face Dee. "I don't believe we've met," he said politely, extending his right hand. "I'm Harry Lockwood."

"We've met," Dee said bitterly.

"I'm sorry. I'm sure I would remember someone as pretty as you," Harry said pleasantly.

"You can't pull this," Dee cried. She turned to Munroe. "This man kidnapped me last night and took me to a shack in the cove."

Munroe looked at Harry questioningly. "Well?"

"Whoa. Hold on, miss," Harry said, taking a step back. "I was home all last night. Where did you say this alleged kidnapping occurred?"

Dee started to answer. But she didn't want to admit she had been in Harry's attic. She decided to ignore the question. "You pushed me, and I hit my head," she said.

"That's a very nasty bump," Harry replied

softly, sounding concerned. "You should get out of the cold and have a doctor look at that. You know, it's very common for people with head injuries to have some pretty strange ideas—hallucinations, even."

"Stop acting so innocent," Dee cried, her voice at least an octave higher than usual. "You tied me up in a fish net and left me there after I saw you steal your mother's coin collection. You have those coins right in that briefcase."

Harry didn't show the slightest sign of guilt or fear. The smile never left his face. "I have nothing but business papers in here," he said, holding up the case. Turning to Munroe, he added, "If you have a proper search warrant, I'll be glad to show them to you, although I think you'd find them very boring."

"Never mind that," Munroe said impatiently. "What about the other charges? Did you kidnap this girl and tie her up in that shack by the cove?"

"Let me just ask her a question or two, Munroe," Harry said quietly. "Did I tie you up tightly?" he asked Dee.

"Of course you did!" Dee screamed. "I couldn't move! I could have been there for days!"

"Well then," Harry said, his smile widening, "if I tied you up so tightly, how did you get away?"

"I—uh . . ." Dee was stuck. She couldn't tell them that Louisa had helped her escape.

"Yes. How *did* you get away, dear?" Aunt Win asked, looking doubtful for the first time.

"I . . . I just did!" Dee cried. "But that's not important. What's important is that I was in Mrs. Lockwood's attic, and I saw him—"

"You broke into my mother's attic?" Harry sounded shocked. "I thought I heard noises up there last night." Then his voice turned threatening as he added, "Listen, if anything is missing, I think the police will know who to question first."

"Is this true?" Munroe asked, turning his attention back to Dee. "You broke into the Lockwoods' attic?"

"Well . . . not exactly." Dee felt so frustrated. Why wouldn't anyone believe her?

"Can I go now, Munroe?" Harry asked quietly. "I really think you should get this girl to a doctor. And I have a business meeting on the mainland that I'm already late for."

"Yeah. Sure. Go ahead," Munroe said, staring at Dee. "I don't see any reason to keep you."

"I hope the young lady feels better soon," Harry said. Then giving Aunt Win a sympathetic look, he turned and walked down the dock toward the ferry, jauntily swinging the attaché case.

CHAPTER
20

He's getting away, Dee thought in despair. But Harry was still a few yards from the ferry when he appeared to trip over nothing at all. He let out a cry of surprise as he fell forward, flat on his face. His attaché case flew out of his hands and landed on its side on the dock.

A few seconds later, as if by magic, the two latches snapped open. The lid popped up, revealing a black velvet pouch inside. The pouch tilted over—and a stream of gold coins poured out into the case.

Way to go, Louisa! Dee cried to herself.

With a look of total astonishment, Harry

pulled himself up and frantically moved to close the attaché case. But he was too late.

"Those don't look like business papers to me," Munroe said, walking purposefully toward Harry.

"They're Mrs. Lockwood's coins. I told you!" Dee cried happily.

"How in the world did you know?" Aunt Win exclaimed.

"Stand back, Munroe. I'm getting on the ferry—with this case," Harry growled, dropping all pretense.

"I'm afraid I have to ask you to stay until we get this little matter cleared up," Munroe said. He reached for the pistol in the holster at his waist.

With a cry of desperation, Harry picked up the attaché case and flung it at Munroe. It hit the constable in the stomach, and he doubled over in pain.

Forgetting the coins, Harry ran past the groaning Munroe and headed for the woods on the other side of the road. "Stop him! He's getting away!" Dee cried.

But there was someone waiting for Harry on the other side of the street. The ragged-looking man, Harry's brother, made a flying tackle, bringing Harry to the ground with a grunt of pain and surprise.

"William, you idiot! Let me go!" Harry screamed.

"You're not going anywhere," William said, holding his squirming brother on the ground. "I was there last night. I saw what you did."

Munroe, still clutching his stomach, hurried over to them. "Well, well . . . the black sheep of the Lockwood family," he said to William. "I thought you were still in prison for that California stock swindle. What brings you back to Misty Island?"

"I served my time. I've been back for a while," William told Munroe. "I found the girl in the shack last night. She seemed okay, so I came here to try and stop Harry before getting help for her."

"Looks like you stopped him all right," Munroe said.

"Dee, how did you get involved in all this?" Aunt Win asked.

"It's a long story," Dee sighed.

"It may have been a long story, but it's just about over now," Munroe said, pulling Harry to his feet. "Come on. I think it's time we paid your mother a visit."

* * *

Mrs. Lockwood was so surprised to see them all, she nearly dropped the potted orchid she was holding. But the surprises were just beginning for her.

The most unhappy surprise was seeing the gold coins in Harry's suitcase. "Those were your father's," she told Harry sadly. "I didn't even know they were in the house. I thought they were safely locked in a vault at the bank."

Harry couldn't look his mother in the eye.

Mrs. Lockwood glared at her son. "I'm glad your father didn't live to see this," she said, shaking her head sadly.

"Are you going to press charges?" Munroe asked, putting his big hand on Harry's shoulder.

"Oh, no. I couldn't do that," Mrs. Lockwood said. "After all, he *is* my son." She turned to Harry. "But I want you out of this house—now. I won't have a common thief living under my roof."

"I'll watch him while he packs his things," Munroe said. "And I'll make sure that's *all* he packs!"

Harry walked slowly up to his room with Munroe following close behind.

As soon as they were gone, Mrs. Lockwood

turned to William. She couldn't seem to believe he was actually there. "Look at you— you're a sight," she scolded, tears spilling down her cheeks. "Where have you been, William? I knew your prison term was over. Why didn't you ever come home?"

William's face paled with emotion. "I sent you a note saying I was back," he said. "You never even bothered to reply. I couldn't believe my own mother didn't want to see me. I sent you another note. But you didn't answer that one, either. So I stayed away." He looked down at the floor.

"But I never got any notes from you!" his mother cried.

"Of course you did," William insisted. "I gave them to Harry."

"Harry!" Mrs. Lockwood cried as she realized what must have happened. "He never gave them to me. Of course he didn't want you around. He was afraid you might interfere with his plans to steal from his own family."

"Well, I'm back now," William said, rushing into his mother's open arms. When they finished hugging, they both had tears running down their cheeks.

"We should be going," Aunt Win said uncomfortably, tugging at Dee's arm.

"I'm sorry. I nearly forgot you were here. So much excitement!" Mrs. Lockwood said, keeping an arm around William's shoulder.

"I'm glad it worked out so well," Dee said.

"So am I," Mrs. Lockwood agreed, smiling at her son. "Dee, I understand you're responsible for . . . for everything."

"Well, really, I—" Dee started.

"There's no way I can ever repay you for returning my son to me," Mrs. Lockwood said gratefully. "But I would like to give you some token of my appreciation. Is there something special you would like—one of my prize orchids perhaps?"

"You don't have to give me anything," Dee protested. "I'm glad I was able to help." But when Mrs. Lockwood insisted, Dee had a sudden idea.

"Well, actually, there is something I'd like." She turned to William. "In the shack at Fingers Cove, I saw an old Bible with a Lockwood family tree in it. Do you think I could have that?"

"Why, Dee!" Aunt Win cried, surprised. "What on earth for?"

"For . . . this project I'm doing," Dee replied.

"Of course you can have it," William told Dee with a smile. "I'll bring it to the inn this afternoon. But are you sure that's all you want?"

"Oh, yes. Thank you!" Dee cried.

Mrs. Lockwood gave her a hug, and minutes later Dee and her aunt were back in the jeep. Dee immediately rested her head against the seatback and closed her eyes. She could feel Louisa's presence, right behind her.

Dee didn't say a word all the way home. And as soon as Aunt Win pulled the jeep up to the inn, Dee ran inside and headed up to her room. "Where are you going?" Aunt Win called after her.

"Upstairs to change out of these filthy, wet clothes," Dee said.

The minute Dee closed the bedroom door behind her, Louisa slowly began to materialize. This time, her happy smile was the first thing to appear. "We did it, Louisa!" Dee cried. "Isn't it wonderful?"

"Yes, it is wonderful," Louisa said. "I'm truly happy, Dee, and very encouraged."

"You *should* be!" Dee exclaimed. "You helped

two relatives this morning—Mrs. Lockwood and William. Only two more to go!"

"And with the family tree from that Bible, I'm sure we'll be able to find a whole lot of my relations!" Louisa said. Both girls couldn't stop grinning at each other. Louisa looked happier than Dee had ever seen her.

"Dee, dear, come on down!" Aunt Win called from the kitchen. "I've made us some hot chocolate!"

Dee gave Louisa a quick hug, then quickly changed her clothes and hurried downstairs.

"Drink it while it's still warm," Aunt Win said, plopping two large white mugs on the checkered tablecloth.

Dee sat down across from her aunt. For a long while, they both sat in silence, watching the steam rise from their mugs.

Finally, Aunt Win said, "Dee, do you want to explain everything that happened now?"

Dee thought hard. "Yes," she said. "I guess I'd better start at the very beginning, Aunt Win. You see, when I first arrived here, I discovered a ghost up in my room. Her name is Louisa and she's the same age as me, except that she died in 1897. She's invisible most of the time and—"

Aunt Win threw up her hands. "Okay, okay," she groaned, rolling her eyes. "If you don't want to tell me the real story, that's fine with me!"

Dee gave her aunt a dazzling smile. Then she took a long, soothing sip of the hot chocolate.

"Delicious," Dee said.

Coming Soon: **THE MYSTERY OF MISTY ISLAND INN**

In Book II of *Haunting with Louisa*, Dee and Louisa are enjoying a walk on Misty Island when something unexpected happens. Here's a scene from *The Mystery of Misty Island Inn*:

Thwap! A big, soft snowball skidded off the side of Dee's shoulder. It hit the road and bounced back up. With disbelieving eyes, Dee watched it roll across the road and settle on the other side. She ran over to retrieve it and laughed as she picked up a small rubber ball that had been covered with snow.

"Throw it back," a high-pitched young voice demanded. A blond boy of seven or eight was standing in the front yard of a gray, weather-beaten house just off the road. "Throw it back," he repeated. "It's mine."

Dee brushed the remaining snow off the ball and hurled it as hard as she could. The boy jumped up and caught it, then came running toward her. "Just a few more throws," he pleaded. "There's no one to play with. I'm bored."

"Let's add a little excitement to this boy's day," Dee whispered to Louisa.

"What do you mean?" Louisa's disembodied voice replied.

"I have an idea," Dee said. "I'll show you." She held up her hands to the boy. "Let me see that ball."

When he tossed it to her, Dee pretended to examine the ball. "Just as I thought," she said. "This is a very special ball."

"Huh?" he asked, stopping at the edge of his yard.

"Yup. It's a boomerang ball," Dee told him, struggling to keep a straight face.

"What's that?" the boy asked skeptically.

"I'll show you," Dee said, stepping up from the road into his front yard. "Now watch. I'm going to throw the ball as hard as I can. It's going to stop in midair and then come flying back to me."

The boy laughed scornfully. "That's dumb. A ball can't do that."

"This one can," Dee insisted. "It will almost seem as if an invisible person had caught it and thrown it back," she added pointedly, wanting to be sure Louisa understood her part in the little trick. Then Dee took the ball with a flourish and tossed it across the yard. It went about thirty feet and then stopped, hovering unnaturally in midair before it came flying back to her.

"Wow!" cried the boy. "It really *is* a boomerang ball! Can I try?"

"Go ahead," Dee said, handing it to him.

The boy pulled his arm back and threw the ball. It sailed up into a high arc. Dee knew he had tossed it way over Louisa's head. But suddenly the ball stopped high in the sky. Again it hovered and then came sailing back to the boy.

"We can do this all day!" cried the boy.

"Uh, I'm afraid not. You see, the ball is only good for exactly ten throws," Dee bluffed. "Then it conks out."

The boy continued to throw the ball. Several of his throws were wild, and Dee was sure Louisa would miss them. But each time the ball stopped and then came back. Finally Dee called a halt to the game. "That's ten," she announced. "The ball has used up all its power."

Unconvinced, the boy tossed the ball again. This time it landed with a *plunk* in the wet snow. "Aw," he said disappointed. But then his face brightened. "Wait till the other kids hear about this!"

"See, it wasn't such a boring day after all." Dee laughed. She waved good-bye to the boy and headed back down to the road, still smiling. The boy continued to wave until she rounded the bend and was out of sight.

"Well, that was fun," Louisa said, coming into view again. "I never used to be very good at playing ball," she admitted.

"You were catching that ball like a pro today."

Louisa smiled. "Yes. Well, being able to do this helps." And as she spoke, she floated up into the air until her sneakers were level with Dee's astonished gaze.

"Louisa, stop that!" Dee cried sharply, looking quickly up and down the road. "Someone is going to see you."

Laughing lightly, Louisa settled to the

ground. "There's no one here," she said with a grin.

But suddenly Louisa stopped short. She clutched Dee's wrist with one hand while the other pointed shakily at the deserted guest house. "Oh, my soul!" she gasped. "It's him!"

Dee looked toward the house. At the window stood a tall, thin man, staring out at them. In the next second he stepped back into the shadows of the room and seemed to disappear. But not before Dee got a look at his unearthly pale face and glowing green eyes. "Who is he?" Dee asked Louisa urgently.

Louisa continued to stare at the vacant window. "It's him," she repeated. "He said he'd come to get me and he has. Matthew Duncan's come back from beyond the grave!"

Dee is shocked. Is this man really a ghost? Why would he want to hurt Louisa? And what is there about Louisa's past that Dee doesn't know?

ABOUT THE AUTHOR

EMILY CATES was born in New York City but she spent her summers on the coast of Maine, which gave her the inspiration for the Haunting with Louisa trilogy. She has written several books for adults and has published poetry in several journals. *The Ghost in the Attic* is her first book for young readers. Ms. Cates now divides her time between Boston, Massachusetts, and Block Island, which is very much like Misty Island in the Haunting with Louisa trilogy.

Scare yourself with spooky books by

John Bellairs!

Read them all...if you dare.

Creaky stairs...bumps in the night...ghosts and wizards and mummies! Each one of these terrific books is spine-tingling, thrilling and chillingly scary!

☐ 15697-7 **The Lamp From The Warlock's Tomb** $2.95

☐ 15540-7 **The Curse Of The Blue Figurine** $2.95

☐ 15621-7 **The Dark Secret Of Weatherend** $2.95

☐ 15552-0 **The Eyes Of The Killer Robot** $2.95

☐ 15701-9 **The Mummy, The Will, And The Crypt** $2.95

☐ 15451-6 **The Revenge Of The Wizard's Ghost** $2.75

☐ 15726-4 **The Spell Of The Sorcerer's Skull** $2.95

☐ 15629-2 **The Treasure Of Alpheus Winterborn** $3.50

<u>Prices and availability subject to change without notice</u>

Bantam Books, Dept. SK36, 414 East Golf Road, Des Plaines, IL 60016

Please send me the items I have checked above. I am enclosing $_____
(please add $2.00 to cover postage and handling). Send check or money
order, no cash or C.O.D.s please.

Mr/Ms _____

Address _____

City/State _____ Zip _____

SK36-9/90

Magical Skylark Adventures!

☐ **THE CASTLE IN THE ATTIC**
by Elizabeth Winthrop   15601 $3.50
William is sure there's something magical about the castle he receives
as a present. When he picks up the tiny silver knight, it comes to life!
Suddenly William is off on a fantastic quest to another land and time—
where a fiery dragon and an evil wizard are waiting to do battle...

☐ **THE PICOLINIS**
by Anne Graham Estern   15566 $2.75
Jessica and Peter Blake are thrilled when their parents buy a wonderful
antique dollhouse. But now they hear noises at night...music and voices
that seem to come from the dollhouse. Are the Picolini dolls alive?
The Blake children embark on an exciting and dangerous adventure
in search of lost treasure.

☐ **THE PICOLINIS AND THE HAUNTED HOUSE**
by Anne Graham Estern   15771 $2.95
Jessica and Peter discover a secret passageway in the house across the street
that thieves have been using for years. Now they want to find the thieves!
Can the Picolini dolls help them?

☐ **THE GHOST WORE GRAY**
by Bruce Coville   15610-1 $2.75
Sixth grader Nina Tanleven and her best friend Chris are visiting
an old country inn when suddenly the ghost of a young confederate soldier
appears! They know he's trying to tell them something. But what?

☐ **THE GHOST IN THE THIRD ROW**
by Bruce Coville   15646-2 $2.95
For Nina Tanleven nothing is scarier than trying out for a part in the school
play...except seeing a ghost sitting in the audience! Soon strange things
begin to happen and it's up to Nina to solve the mystery!

Watch for new Abracadabra books each month!

Buy them at your local bookstore or use this handy coupon for ordering:

Bantam Books, Dept. SK40, 414 East Golf Road, Des Plaines, IL 60016

Please send me the items I have checked above. I am enclosing $____
(please add $2.00 to cover postage and handling). Send check or money
order, no cash or C.O.D.s please.

Mr/Ms _____

Address _____

City/State _____ Zip _____

SK40-10/90

Please allow four to six weeks for delivery.
Prices and availability subject to change without notice.